THE FOURTH WORLD

# The Fourth World

*El cuarto mundo*

DIAMELA ELTIT

Translated & with a Foreword

BY DICK GERDES

University of Nebraska Press

Lincoln and London

Originally published as *El cuarto mundo*, ©
Diamela Eltit, 1988

© 1995 by the University of Nebraska Press

All rights reserved

Manufactured in the United States of America. The paper in this
book meets the minimum requirements of
American National
Standard for Information Sciences – Permanence of Paper for
Printed Library Materials, ANSI Z39.48-1984.

Library of Congress Cataloging-in-Publication Data

Eltit, Diamela, 1949–

*[Cuarto mundo. English]* The fourth world / Diamela
Eltit; translated and
with a foreword by Dick Gerdes. p. cm.–(Latin American women writers)

ISBN 0-8032-1817-6 (alk. paper).–ISBN 0-8032-6723-1
(pbk.: alk. paper)

I. Gerdes, Dick. II. Title. III. Series. PQ8098.15.L78C813
1995 863–dc20 95-2428 CIP

# Contents

# Translator's Foreword

CHILE has witnessed a spectacular transition from the Latin American country best known for fostering poets such as Nobel Prize for Literature recipients Gabriela Mistral and Pablo Neruda to producing fiction writers who have acquired a notable presence not only in Chile but also in the international arena. The writings of José Donoso (b. 1924), Antonio Skarmeta (b. 1940), Ariel Dorfman (b. 1942), Isabel Allende (b. 1942), and Diamela Eltit (b. 1949) have been translated and read with enthusiasm in several languages, including French, German, Italian, and English. Diamela Eltit is the newcomer to this family of seasoned writers, and she is one of the most intellectual, creative, innovative, challenging, and unsettling of this group.

One key to appreciating the strange worlds of Eltit's writings is to realize that while those other writers fled into exile after a 1973 military takeover of Salvador Allende's Marxist government in Chile (Allende was killed in the coup), Diamela Eltit, then twenty-four years old, found no alternative but to join resistance groups and actively protest the newly installed military dictatorship that lasted until 1989 when General César Augusto Pinochet once again allowed democratic elections. Eltit experienced firsthand the devastating effects of dictatorship and what it meant to be a Latin American woman living in exile within her own country during the 1970s.

The mastery of Eltit's fiction is explicit in the way she handles language. In her novels, narrative discourse is not shaped by conventional storytelling techniques or standard characterizations, but rather by the utilization of language and syntax to reflect the fragmented and distorted society in which she lived. Hence, Eltit's fiction (fragmentation, violence, and exploitation) is a faithful representation of her life (dictatorship, oppression, and exploitation). It represents symbolically and physically the sociopolitical situation during almost two decades of cruelty in Chile as well as several centuries of foreign domination and exploitation in Latin America. Her writing must be read as a type of literary politics in which linguistic and literary devices require the reader to rethink the novel genre and reconsider its relationship to society.

Diamela Eltit is a professor of literature, film director, cultural activist, and feminist. She presently resides in Chile. Her books question society's dominant structures of power; they look beyond conventional political tools of social analysis and seek to transgress outmoded world order by dismantling, in clinical fashion, language that drives wedges between the sexes. In addition, she attempts to vindicate social marginality produced by the oppression of women, ethnic groups, and the dispossessed in today's society. The titles of her works provide an initial clue to what her narrative worlds signify: *Lumpérica* (1982), *Por la patria* (1986; For the nation), *El cuarto mundo* (1988; *The Fourth World*), *Vaca sagrada* (1991; Sacred cow), and *El padre mío* (1989; My father). *El padre mío* is a testimony based on taped discussions that Eltit conducted with an individual who was once influential but after being subjected to political persecution went insane and became a street person. This text is read less for its literary value than for its psychologically charged presentation of corruption in the Chilean political underworld through the eyes of a mentally deranged person beset by delusions, paranoia, and fear. The title 'My Father' ironically alludes to cultural values based on the concepts of patriarchy, religion, and power that continually lead to corruption, pain, and destruction. Similarly, the title of Eltit's latest novel, 'Sacred Cow,' incorporates cultural symbols that run the gamut from sexual attributes (large-breasted women) to entities often unreasonably immune from criticism or opposition – dictators and politics. Ambiguity is transformed into rebellion when concepts of patriarchy, machismo, exploitation, and power become the suggestive link.

The title of Eltit's first novel, *Lumpérica,* is most likely a combination of 'lumpen' (literally, the dispossessed and uprooted individuals cut off from the economic and social class with which they might normally be identified) and 'America' (meaning, here, the ostracized, illegitimate, inferior world that Latin America – the female – represents from a Spanish, Euro-centered, male perspective). In this case, the combination of these into *Lumpérica* allows for the signified (a vast community of poor undesirables) to be vindicated and to acquire a united voice. (In the United States, a similar process occurred when Hispanic Americans politically empowered themselves by assuming the label 'Chicano,' a term that is used in Mexico with derision against the 'traitors' who went North, similar to the term 'sudaca' in Eltit's novel, used by Spaniards to denigrate Latin Americans.) Finally, *The Fourth World* offers a similar interpretation, even though the narrative process differs somewhat from the other novels. 'The Fourth World' is a recently coined phrase referring to the marginalization of inferiors who are beginning to appear en masse throughout the developed (First) World.

Diamela Eltit has conceived a highly intellectual but carved-in-the-flesh strategy, fusing the political problems of the real world with the aesthetics of literature that wounds, literature with meaning, literature that creates vantage points for understanding society and its problems. Eltit's phantasmagoric worlds provide a cultural analysis neither Formalist nor Marxist, but one that focuses on a systematic and dynamic social language, and one that possesses its own body politic and provides links to diverse human relationships in modern society.

*The Fourth World* has been conceived and brought to life through a series of opposing views that, on one level, demonstrate the violence and exploitation in society, especially when myths, ritual, and habit are at the heart of humankind's problems. On another level, however, in almost post-Hegelian fashion, gender-based opposites (male/female respectively) such as mind/body, exterior/interior, open, public spaces/closed, private spaces, violence/ peace, torture/pleasure, guilt/innocence apparently collide but never really cancel each other out or meld to create a new identity but somehow exist in relation to and for the mere sake of their opposite. The text is divided into two parts: the first, narrated by the male offspring of a set of twins, takes the reader from conception to his teen years and focuses on the mother's pain, delusions, vices, and fears. The second part, narrated by the female twin counterpart, is a vastly different text describing the impending birth of a deformed baby girl (emblematic of the novel itself and all Latin American fiction) conceived incestuously by the twins who, in turn, are abandoned by their parents. Language use in both parts is revealing. The male's discourse can be seen as indirect, winding, nonconfrontational, thoughtful, connoting superiority (as it is with physical space inside the womb: he is on top of her). The female voice tends to be more direct but private, showing emotion, anger, excitement, and passion as she interacts with others (parents, brother, and sister).

The ramifications are varied, but in every situation of the novel the reader is provided new perspectives on old problems: in terms of gender, androgyny; in terms of the politics of oppression, vindication; and in terms of language, symbolism. And there you have it: a tale of sex, politics, and writing; yet sex is perverse (but inescapable), politics are exploitative (and menacing), and writing is an incestuous (but, in the end, vindicating) process.

The nuclear element that provides Eltit the opportunity to fuse sex, politics, and writing is found in the most basic driving force that she knows and viscerally understands: the female body. But it is the female body that is wounded and pained not only by menstruation, coitus, incest, rape, childbirth, sickness, and old age, but also by the hidden violence existing in every couple. It is the female body of political marginality (hence, the term 'sudaca' in the novel) writing from a position of inferiority, deformity, ambiguity, irony, and anarchy, all of which place Eltit squarely within a challenging, revolutionary perspective. And while the future looks ominous, the novel also speaks for battered, sick bodies which are, once and for all, redeemed. There is no doubt that Diamela Eltit is aware that her narratives unmask cultural biases and assume the power inherent in literary works and critical practices.

# 1. DEFEAT WILL BE IRREVOCABLE

ON APRIL 7 my mother woke up with a fever. Sweating and fatigued, she moved between the sheets closer to my father ever so painfully, hoping he would come to her aid. Inexplicably and without compunction, my father possessed her, forcing her to submit to his desires. He was awkward and slow, at moments about to give up, but then he would begin anew, driven by lust.

My mother was conspicuously faint from her fever. Her body was exhausted and irritatingly apathetic. Nothing was said. As my father dominated her with his movements, her only reaction was to comply, automatically and clumsily.

Afterward, when it was over, my mother stretched out between the sheets, falling asleep instantly. Then she had a dream infested with feminine horror.

On that April 7, enshrouded in my mother's fever, I not only was conceived, but also must have shared her dream because I suffered the horrible feminine attack of dread.

THE NEXT DAY, April 8, my mother's condition had deteriorated noticeably. Her sunken eyes and incoherent words meant the fever was rising. Her joints ached, making it severely difficult for her to move. Although she was consumed by thirst, she could not swallow anything. Like her cotton shirt soaking from sweat, her hair was wet and stuck to the sides of her face, causing a rash. While her half-shut eyes filtered out the light entering the room, her feverish body trembled spasmodically.

Gloomily, my father just stood by and watched her. No doubt because he was terrified, in the morning he possessed her again – hurriedly, ineptly, demanding little. Seemingly unaware of anything around her, she only complained of an intense numbing pain in her legs that my father, by rubbing them, tried to alleviate.

Like the day before, she fell asleep quickly and began to dream again, but this time her dream was fraught with strange, obscure images, like an erupting volcano with gushing lava.

My mother's dream reached me in flashes: even though the gush of red lava frightened me, I rejoiced, for I felt as if I were witnessing a divine ritual.

Before long, I understood the two opposing sensations; after all, it was simple and predictable: on that April, my father engendered my twin sister.


I REACTED to perturbing and chaotic emotions that day. The intrusion into my space became unbearable, but it was irrevocable.

My world was relatively calm at first, despite vague sensations of malaise that I could never completely repress. We were but larvae swept along by the waters, our two cords helping us to live in quasi-independent spaces.

But that illusion was always short-lived because of the frequency of my mother's dreams, which were patterned after two merging symmetrical figures – two spires, two panthers, two old people, two roads.

Those dreams would make me nervous, but the tension would eventually dissipate. My trepidation would be transformed into an infernal hunger, forcing me to satiate myself by opening corporeal floodgates that were not yet ready to perform such tasks.

Afterward, I would be overcome by lethargy, sometimes confused with a state of serenity. Still fraught with indecision, however, I would let my senses flow outward.

WITH HER health restored, my mother not only returned to her normal routine, but demonstrated a surprising propensity for the ordinary: there was more laughter than tears, more activity than rest, more doing than thinking.

To tell the truth, my mother had few ideas and her lack of originality irritated me the most. She would simply follow my father's ideas and, fearing that she might annoy him, would never question him.

Curiously, she showed considerable interest in her body; she was constantly wanting to go out and buy dresses, exclusive perfumes, even garish adornments. When she walked, my mother's ample yet supple body would sway rhythmically, giving the impression of robust good health. Perhaps it was the unusualness of her infirmity that made my father's loins burn when he saw her for the first time, helpless and diminished; not as a corporal other, but more like a mass of captive, submissive flesh.

WITHOUT ANY particular reason, I think that routine might have allowed me to separate myself from my twin sister, who was always lingering nearby. Even without wanting to be near her, I was still unable to avoid her movements and intentions. Early on, I was able to detect her true nature and, more important, her feelings toward me.

While I struggled with my apprehensions, she had to cope with her obsessions. As she began to grow, she would unleash innumerable, mysterious pulsations.

Her obsessions began the very moment she was conceived, the moment she began to anguish over the real dimension and precise significance of my presence. Immediately, she began seeking me out, but I evaded her, of course, keeping as much distance between us as possible.

During that first period, life was rudimentary: I would always be attuned to the movement of the waters, and when they became agitated I would chart a course taking me in the opposite direction.

My sister was weaker than me, which, of course, was due to the chronology oỉ our conception; nevertheless, the differences between us were still greatly disproportionate. It seemed as though my mother's debility and my father's lack of vigor during sex had caused her weakness.

In my case, I benefited from my sister's fragility, for movements fatigued her and greatly reduced her radius of action.

Shortly thereafter, she began to trap me with her little tricks: every time I moved, the currents of the jostling waters would push her forward and, on two occasions, she crashed into me. I remember these moments as offensive, even threatening.

I had to confront her obsessions directly – the same ones I had been ignoring until that time – and while they would last barely an instant, there was something remarkably intimate about them. Nevertheless, after those two encounters I began to understand my strange sensation of her complicity with my mother.

I EXERCISED my utmost capacity to think. Before, I struggled with impressions that I would transform into truths, realizing later that none of it was very surprising.

The knowledge that my mother was my sister's accomplice enervated me, yet it was imperative to disentangle the form and meaning of such an alliance.

I didn't understand much, except that the two times my sister collided with me, she, not I, held the answer to two of my mother's dreams. The explanations, of course, were intolerable and constraining. After having been precariously excluded, I tracked my mother's every move.

MY MOTHER, after some time, began to display such subtle, ambiguous changes that I began to see them as a product of my uneasy interpretations. Nevertheless, she was changing.

For some mysterious reason, she had created a barrier between us, which hurt me deeply and left me feeling vulnerable. However, as soon as I understood that I was the source of her panic, my fears were placated.

My mother, who was afraid of me, created a strange relationship between us, and it seemed as if she could only become her true self with my sister.

Cognizant of events happening around me, I discovered that my mother would lie to my father, a behavior that she had learned well and which was simply a strategic move to perpetuate his illusion of power.

While I should have figured it out from the beginning, especially given the nature of her dreams, I had let myself be deceived by her apparent sincerity. Frankly, she was indifferent to wearing apparel or jewelry; it was my father who imposed his desires on her. By consciously submitting to them, she hoped to not only please him but also humiliate him.

I also discovered that my mother's thoughts were tinged with fantasies that prompted strong guilt and, at times, triggered excessively hard self-punishment.

Often she would not eat, fasting for several days at a time. Then her fantasies would subside significantly, yet she was always haunted by less pernicious ones, like running away or craving exotic food. However, once the effect of her dieting would wear off, she would give in to fantasizing again, which would initiate the painful process all over again.

Another one of her methods consisted of taking on tasks that she hated to do, but those same tasks would receive her fullest attention. Volunteering to help sick elderly people, she would wash their feet with her own hands and, in that way, be completely open to her fears of catching a contagious disease. Afterward, she purposely avoided cleansing herself of the odor that had penetrated her skin.

While my father did not approve of her dieting, he did admire her for her volunteer work, especially the time she devoted to blind children housed in state institutions on the outskirts of the city. He derived great pleasure from listening to her describe their world in detail, which, in turn, stimulated my mother, surprisingly, to provide accurate descriptions. She could even identify many of them by name; in fact, she was able to describe each child with precision.

She explained how she would clean out the children's hollow eye sockets, mere festering cavities of pus. My father looked at her with admiration, but she acted as if helping the blind meant nothing to her.

There is no doubt that my mother detested those visits because the children, who were fascinated by the smell of her perfume, would throw themselves upon her, pulling at her clothes, even scratching her. Euphoric, they would run into the walls, causing much hilarity among the others. On those occasions my mother would shudder upon hearing their primitive, guttural sounds.

She kept those reactions – and her constant feelings of repulsion – to herself. But my sister and I, who were a part of our mother's dark, creative recesses, would experience her stories like frightening premonitions. Confined to this closed system in which we were living, it was terribly hard to relate to her stories. Disconnected and enveloped in darkness, my sister would tremble with fear; and I would control my impulses by seeking her for protection. On those occasions, to be close to each other would partially alleviate our perpetual fear of oblivion.

UNEXPECTEDLY, my mother abandoned her charitable activities while at the same time, amid alarming confusion, her body underwent a transformation that overpowered her for several days. We would frequently feel her hand touching her tense, stretched skin, probing herself, caught between obsession and dread.

Her fantasy world came to an end, however, and she began to focus her attention on impossible tasks, such as attempting to visualize the biological process going on inside herself, hoping in the process to dispel feelings of expropriation. As always, the project was a deceptive attempt to permeate us with guilt.

Like a waxy mass, our feelings of guilt grew within our confined waters, but we were able to invert the process upon discovering we had the capability of inventing her dreams, those aquatic dreams contrived with the imagery of a fractured reality. Our dreams were fused, yet ludicrously abstract, not unlike a severe neurological breakdown.

Living in a state of agitation, my mother lost a good part of her hair, and almost lost control of half of her face and the capacity to focus at a distance.

We didn't plan it that way, it was spontaneous, yet it cost me dearly, for I had to give in to my sister's pressures.

Even though I was repulsed by her oppression, I allowed her to approach me and, when we rubbed together, she would rant and rave with envy. I cannot say when exactly she understood how we differed from each other; it might have been the third or fourth time we bumped into each other, or when I felt her quivering so hard that the turbulent waters hurled me against the surrounding walls. Unable to recover in time, I felt her approach me again, with such frightening impulses, and rub impudently against my incipient but already established modesty.

Feeling harassed but not knowing why, I tried to push her away, but the friction of her obsessive rubbing back and forth paralyzed me. I surmised that it was preferable to let her satiate her curiosity, which would allow us to define our battle lines, but suddenly my sister became motionless, even strangely passive. As she held me at bay, for the first time she revealed her intentions to me.

MY MOTHER decided to resolve her differences with our shameless dreams in a friendly way. Learning to share fraternal cohesion and how to deal with her initial opposition, she all but came to enjoy those sensations. Along with the dreams, she also learned to accept the fact that there was nothing more typically unyielding than human nature.

Although I was upset over the changes in her, I resigned myself to her new behavior out of laziness. However, I had substituted my anger for conformity too quickly; her suddenly unstable existence precluded enjoying any kind of stability. I had come to understand that my mother was totally capable of letting everything go, including herself, whenever she faced even the most distant threat.

This situation was directly related to my father. His attitude toward beauty was disconcerting. Now he avoided my mother, for she had become the perfect example of the folly of the feminine condition. Detached, frightened, and secretive, he was repulsed not only by her irregular, painful movements when she walked, but also by the evil that shone from her face.

Once my mother understood perfectly what was happening, she felt complacent and free, for through him, finally, she discovered the real feeling of rejection which, in turn, allowed her to justify her own hatred.

She approached him with all kinds of unacceptable demands. The possibility of sleeping together was untenable, and she didn't attempt to defend herself with excuses.

Having attained the full scope of his masculinity, he became intolerant of any other form of independent fertilization. This proved my mother's old intuitions. She saw herself floating in the universe of loneliness, condemned to tormenting, alien failure.

LITTLE BY LITTLE, the circumscribed space allocated to us was beginning to shrink. There was no alternative but to let our bodies rub against each other. With the illusion of independence no longer imaginable, I could see that the lack of space around us would get worse, making it impossible to move in the surrounding waters.

It was not fair having to share the consequences of enclosure with someone else, or being subjected to an abnormal, exasperating triangle. I was forced to accept not only my body, moist with deep red substances on the inside, but also a body that was growing next to me on the outside. All of my impulses extended well beyond normal limits. The feminine counterparts, which were dominant in this situation, carried persistent messages. Trying to escape her desperation was impossible; so, instead, I opted for openly imposing my masculinity.

Soon I was facing the saturation point; despite our attempts to change positions, the space would not contain us any longer. One last, humiliating option was open to us: my sister maneuvered herself to a position underneath me, which only increased the pressure. We began to suffer, and due to the pain that we were sharing, we reached our first mutual understanding.

MY MOTHER thought about death, but the pain she was suffering prevented a catastrophe. Her back felt like it was practically splitting down the middle and the expression on her face, covered in a rash, revealed excruciating pain whenever she tried to move.

She would think about death as the final phase of her biological undertaking and, strangely, she was ever so serene about it. She firmly believed that every mistake, every detestable act of her life, would receive adequate retribution because of her relentless suffering. She was also steadfast in her belief that she was giving up her body in exchange for her soul. Suffering from the pain, her flesh had paid for her wrongdoing.

Her heart, pounding rapidly, thumping hard and even skipping beats, seemed to sound a death knell. Isolated by her eternal loneliness, my mother became overly conscious of the passage of time, resulting in her rejection of our existence from the very moment she decided to envelop us in her sacrificial ceremony.

Her travels through life, she thought, would not be tarnished if she died honestly. While her death would change nothing, do nothing, her existence was only as real as the rugged vitality of her body. So, we were nothing more than instruments precipitating her own cannibalism. She could feel that her own gestating creation was destroying her.

WE EXPERIENCED the feeling of limits for the first time. Immobilized in the amniotic waters, my sister suffered from my weight on top of her, and I was pressed against the walls, pushing down on top of her.

We were provoked into trying to survive at all costs; instinctively, my sister tried to flee by placing her head in the tunnel. Our world turned to chaos, enmeshed in organic turmoil and cellular revolt. My mother's entire physiology was put on alert: blood began to trickle down through the opening.

My sister lashed out with fury, pounding hard against the stubbornness of her mother's bones. I was alarmed, too, and in response to my sister's panic, I doubled up and awaited the dramatic spectacle. As the hemorrhaging preceded by a terrible echo engulfed me, her violent act dashed my hope for an alliance.

My sister's wild behavior seized me with fear. I thought that both our bodies would be destroyed in the violence. The tension kept mounting for hours. I could feel my sister becoming separated from me, lost in the blood. Not daring to move, I wanted to avoid the red fluid that had enveloped me, but I was carried along by the flow anyway. As I was coming out, I just about suffocated. The hands that clutched me, pulling me out, were the same ones that cut the cord, severing me from my mother's body.

That was the day after my sister had exited. My mother's abrasive legs prepared me for the coarse world of adults.

FORCED to share the same crib, we perceived fragmentary shadows and could hear murmuring around us. While my mother, and her milk, were transmitting permanent feelings of hostility in that unreconcilable environment, my father's astonishment simply added to the ritual.

Having become accustomed to my sister's smell, I detested everything else. For the first time I could actually see her. If my extremities reached out for her but didn't find her in the crib, I would begin to wail, for my fear – seemingly more intense than life itself – was always stronger than my hunger.

She developed a conspicuous affection for touching. On her skin, the touch of a hand or a kiss from moistened lips, gave her much gratification. She had begun to learn to yield not only to me but also to others as well; beforehand, I constituted the lone other.

As I began to feel isolated, everything around me was being reduced to banalities. With the slightest touch, I would feel like dying, for now the other constituted the possible homicidal act of destruction.

My sister liked the affable treatment she received, which awoke a preference for her among those who would invariably compare us. While her seemingly docile nature fascinated everyone, I had become intentionally unsociable, inspiring rejection among those around us.

But my sister hadn't abandoned me for an instant. As she lay next to me, her body was always subordinate to mine, but even then she never felt at ease. Those looks from people who spied on us instigated my shunning of public spheres.

MY MOTHER, weary of having survived the ordeal, reverted back to her old sins. Her ordinary smile signaled her participation in the sacred ritual of our sacrifice.

They gave me the name of my father. They also gave my sister a name. My mother, looking at me deviously, said I was the same as María Chipia, that I was she. Running her slender hand over me, she said: 'You are María Chipia.' A shiver ran down my sister's spine but, gentle as she was, she yielded to the hand touching her head and the name she had received according to ritual. Then my rebellious infirmity became the epicenter of chaos.

Unaware of her desire for revenge, my father contributed to the confusion that my name had created. When he called me, I would turn toward him, not as a way of responding to him but rather to see if he was talking to himself.

Having created a despicable game, my mother wanted to condemn herself irrevocably. But one day love awoke in her with the force of an earthquake. Cleansed by her adoration for us, she took on the look of a young damsel.

Seemingly, peace reigned throughout the house. The encounter with maternal love was her first profound experience in life, and it dazzled her like an adolescent who totters for the first time from the powers of the emotions. But as she assumed her maternal responsibilities, wanting to protect us from the dangerous world around us, she turned all her attention toward us. Even though my sister's illness was brought to a halt, her cells were still carrying her contagious fever.

While she insisted on the legality of my name in order to eliminate its lack of specificity and straightforward human character, I was unable to do it: every time she called out my name while she rocked me in the cradle, I would turn to look at my father.

I soon became dependent upon my self-generated excrement: fascinated by its rhythmic production, I would roll about in it, feeling its soft, warm texture. I yearned to bury myself in it and experience from deep down inside the profound nature of pleasure.

My sister found consolation in her beauty. She learned to transmit her pleasure to others and, in that way, experience pleasure herself. She was an object to be admired as she struggled to make her body exude polished, frivolous perfection. Instinctively, her mind learned the art of anticipation, and she gleaned pleasure from it. In her mad search for love, she fell into hypocrisy, but this habit also developed out of fear, for something had warned her that someone, anyone, even her mother, was preparing not only to attack her but also to destroy her. She imagined being blinded or maimed, all primitive fantasies of torture.

At night her small, spasmodic body would cuddle up to me; nervous, her mouth would suck on me. During those nights that first year I learned about the delicate, complex nature of the young female body. I would become frightened as we rubbed up against each other in the dark, but I also began to think that there was neither one precise place for anyone nor were we each one individual person but, instead, we were each just half of one another, unnaturally complementary, all of which forced me to consider my hybrid nature.

My mother's dreams seemed to thrive on one reckless, feminine mistake: having domesticated us as a single pair, she never made an attempt in her dreams to investigate our genital differences – that unsettling occult rupture found in two roads, two panthers, two old people. Without a doubt, her deep sense of chastity thwarted her from conceiving the terrible differences existing, from the very beginning, between the human couple that we always were.

During the night, while I was feeling trapped by the dependency and naiveté that emanated from the center of my unconsciousness, once again I rubbed up against my sister.

My astute, perceptive body, which was now separate from hers due to the absurdity of her small size, found warmth in hers. Enveloped in drowsiness, she was prudent at first, then savage in her explorations.

MY MOTHER became excited by these new feelings of maternal love, and she began to exaggerate things; ever vigilant, however, she still feared for us.

Now that she had been spared the punishment of death, she imagined she was going to be doubly chastised by our deaths, confusing them with her own. When our cries reached overly strident levels, she would nearly collapse in panic. Her outstretched arms would lift us up and squeeze us hard against her body. Since distrust was another one of her traits, she could never escape from her dreams, abandon food, or even leave the room.

My father had become obnoxious and my mother would not look up to answer his questions. He would occasionally caress us too, but she did everything she could to get him to leave the room so she could continue – alone – watching over us.

At first my father suffered from her obsessions, but he began to ignore her, thinking that it was just another stage and that sooner or later she would return to him – submissive and mute.

Somewhere in the deep recesses of his mind he was proud to see her undertake her maternal responsibilities so meticulously, all of which served to confirm his impression that she was the perfect incarnation of the sensual ancestral woman.

As far as my mother was concerned, my father had no part to play in our lives, except for the simple hellos and goodbyes. In fact, my father meant nothing to her, for he had been neutralized in her memories.

Reminding him of the date she had given birth, she would rely on the old excuse of her health and thereby extend considerably their abstinence.

Repulsed by her marriage obligations, she would remember shamefully, without desire, the brazen and ignoble excesses of the body.

The torment of jealousy had now disappeared, for she knew that my father was imposing his lust on someone else; however, she also confirmed her wretched femininity that, in turn, diminished her maternal status. True, her motherly affection lacked comparison, but she did become confused when she related it to other genital functions.

However, my mother finally found the reality of her sex.

The conflict, frightening and unrelenting, had been resolved through the conventional nature of her role. She lamented having discovered the truth so late and through so much pain. Remembering herself wet with sweat, yearning, and waiting for a response from my father revolted her, leaving her feeling denigrated. She controlled my father's now external and distant range of activity.

Believing sympathetically that he had been deprived of any absolute, permanent pleasure, she had found an explanation for his paternal bifurcation toward trivial but blissful whims that produced an intensity unequaled by alcohol or some other satiating pleasure of the body.

Convinced he would only be able to satiate himself in death, she would be the catalyst for his discovery of his own reality. She, on the other hand, was ascending toward inexplicable heights.

CLASPING HANDS with my sister and curling up around her, I began to whimper, for everything was spinning around diffusely and dizzily. And I even seemed to hover outside my own body. I had a fever.

The fever was less symmetrical to pain than it was to a strange state of suspension in which everything, while possible, was at the same time improbable. As objects seemed to flee from me, I also became mesmerized by the objects surrounding me.

My fever began in the early morning hours, at sunrise. The virulence of the light made things strange as they magically broke into particles, becoming atomized upon reaching my obstructed view. Alarmed by my shivering, my sister squeezed my fingers and moved away slightly in order to give me more room. My illness didn't seem to be an enemy but rather inaccessible and derisive. I wanted to return to my organic center, but all references had been lost, as if my memory had irrevocably disintegrated.

My inability to determine how much time had passed increased with the torrents of light that immobilized everything. I was incommensurably alone and indifferent to my surroundings. Whatever it was that had happened, it happened inside me, synthetically and limitlessly. This double valence prevented me from meditating. Unable to generate any defense mechanism, I took part in the hysterical impression of my mother looking at her sickly, motionless child.

She began to battle my fever while I, paradoxically, abandoned myself to neutrality. The acute, voracious fever followed its course, immune to the efforts of my mother who had used every recourse available to her in order to bring me back to life.

Relegated to the other side of the room, my sister was not the center of attention anymore, but she used every trick possible to call attention to herself. She would alternate between sweet smiles and a sharp, irritating whine that my mother simply ignored. She came to know hunger and the stinging of her excrement and urine.

They put us in separate beds; I went to my mother's room. She slept minimally in order to attend to my needs. Drowsy, I felt myself being rocked to sleep by her incomprehensible, sobbing prayers.

The tangible part of my life was the fever. It dragged me along toward some no man's land, where there was no distinction between night and day, where, in spite of the light that signaled change, my senses perceived light and dark without distinction. It was as if the two forms had coalesced behind my eyelids.

The most precise indication of the existence of the outside world was the presence of my sister. Her clever but desperate performances vaguely stimulated my interest; her prolonged cooing and her incessant gurgling resonated off and on throughout the room both day and night. Sometimes her playful noises would turn irascible, practically driving my mother crazy. She had to begin to speak sternly to my sister, telling her to quiet down.

Crawling on all fours, my sister began to explore the world around her. Her unsure movements, which before had alarmed my mother, motivated a truce between them. Partially observing her from my bed, I saw that she was extraordinarily quick and lively, as if she were some expensive small pet animal.

Angry and jealous, she would spy on me. But I didn't let it upset me: I understood what she was up to from the beginning. Still, I preferred her creeping across the floor and pulling the objects along with her to the other noises she made.

By dawn my fever started to break; it was gone by midmorning. Once again, deep down inside, my anxiety brought on multiple conflicts and doubts, but happiness and pride overtook my mother like a hurricane. She called to my sister who, smiling subserviently, crawled toward us. Her schemes didn't particularly bother me because her behavior was totally transparent. But my sister had prepared a marvelous trick that left me pale with envy and feeling like a failure: she looked at my mother straight in the face and, in clear fashion and without stuttering, spoke her first word.

MY FATHER was unable to conceal his feelings: he felt deceived. While he pampered her in recognition of her achievements, he only gave me scornful glances. Unable to compete, I left him feeling cheated; he believed that some defect of mine had given her a female advantage. The possibility of my having some defect almost devastated him, for he felt unilaterally responsible, even for the origin of his own corporal cells.

Perceiving him the same way I did, my mother alerted herself to the fact that she had to protect me from his disdain. She began to dramatize the strength of my resistance and to compare in different ways each one of my gestures to his.

By inordinately emphasizing my merits, my mother became an expert at expelling my father's paternal fears; although he was unable to appreciate my virtues, he could never deny them.

My sister accelerated her efforts to gain whatever attention she could. Simple, harmless words spewed out of her mouth with amazing ease as she named basic objects and, especially, when she requested water that was never enough.

I decided not to compete with her language ability. I was anxious to start using words in an absolute way, a way in which language would protect me like heavy armor. I was naive in thinking that speaking was a mysterious, transcendental act, capable of giving order to the chaos that surrounded me.

In one way or another, though, I had to distract my parents in order to become fully endowed. I made progress, which satisfied them, by harmonizing my neurological coordination: I stood up and walked directly in front of them.

I was almost a year old when I crossed that room, avoiding my mother's tear-filled eyes.

AFTER THAT first year my sister and I became noticeably detached. The previous period had seemed like the product of my delirious mind. We were practically strangers, except among those for whom it wasn't appropriate. Our closeness, I believed, to which we had been conditioned, had been created by the nebulous origin of my existence. I had confused the density of the waters not only with my sister's body but also with the internal agitation of flesh that embraced me in my mother's dreams.

Now my mother had acquired the appearance of a woman endowed with a great sense of balance, and my father played the heroic protector of our integrity.

My sister exhibited the characteristics of a pampered but continually whining little girl. By rudely and egotistically defending her skimpy possessions, she would close herself off from the others. If we accidentally touched, we would immediately recoil from each other as if something inappropriate had happened; in truth, we were silently, provokingly defiant of each other.

Occasionally I would be cursed by vague dreams in which I would perceive her compulsively clinging to me; but there were never any precise images, only abstract, transitory forms.

I happily accepted my father's name and managed to acquire that long-awaited harmony with my surroundings. After rejecting my old fantasies about transcendence, I yielded to language in a superficial, playful way.

By then, I understood life to be a series of alternating pleasures provided by my mother who worked hard to create a comfortable environment for us. We were living only for the present moment, and that's the way we lived for the first three years. But my mother broke the spell of normalcy when she began to threaten us by playing the victim. My sister, who was the first one to notice that her behavior was changing, became frightened; in response, she began to seek me out only to discover that I thought there was nothing left between us.

While she was pointing at my mother's figure, a sudden swelling appeared on my mother's right leg, but I didn't detect anything unusual. My sister nodded once again toward the spot where she wanted me to look more closely. My amazement was instantaneous, like an unexpected asthma attack that always returned me to some confusingly prior time.

Distraught, we were being pushed headlong one on top of

the other, knowing once again that my sister and I were menacingly indestructible.

MY MOTHER had experienced subsequent encounters with my father, yielding humbly to him without receiving any pleasure from her marital obligations. In spite of the prolonged interval that she had imposed on him, she finally had to give in. No one could figure out why it didn't occur to her that she might get pregnant again; she simply didn't associate such excessive acts with the possibility. She became alarmed, however, when her menstrual cycle was interrupted and, as time passed, she was confronted with the inescapable fact of a new pregnancy. At that point, one could perceive her enduring contradiction. Instead of confirming her maternal impulses, she became filled with horror once she realized how reproachable she was for having surrendered to the whims of those tiny beings that she herself had conceived.

Repulsed by so much sacrifice, she felt she would be incapable of satisfying the needs of a new being that was growing inside her body; but, realizing there was nothing she could do to prevent it, she took refuge in apathy while continuing to comply with her obligations.

The news made my father happy. He had been criticizing my mother for the excessive amount of time she spent with us, and this new child, he thought, would break that obnoxious triangle. He was also pleased with himself because this new act of fatherhood confirmed his patriarchal aspirations.

My mother, who was never able to repress her true feelings, would make faces, which caused him to explode repeatedly with anger and reproach her for her erratic behavior.

My father felt as if he didn't know her anymore, but then he thought that perhaps she needed special attention. The next day he gave her some exquisite perfume. She accepted it, but she never looked up, even though she had apparently recovered from her earlier depression.

As soon as my father smelled her wearing the perfume, he believed that our world had returned to normal. After that, he never gave any more thought to her, except when he would see her looking downtrodden and wandering aimlessly about the house. Although he was overcome with a profound compassion for her animal-like destiny, he also felt doubly happy to be a man, a condition which gave him a stable and illuminating destiny.

AH! HOW demanding my sister and I were during those months! Realizing we had no one but each other, we clung tenaciously to one another in order to deflect any criticism that came our way. Our ancestral pact had definitely brought us together, allowing us to play several unlikely roles: husband and wife, father and daughter, mother and son, brother and sister, friends. Seeking to capture real-life situations, we would play every possible role, from perfect and guilt-ridden parts to hostile and loving ones. We would play until we dropped from exhaustion, then we would begin anew, forming our predestined dyads. We also exchanged roles: if I was the wife, my sister would play the husband while we watched the other rise blissfully to our ideal condition.

During that time, we managed to consolidate our shrewdness while avoiding our mother who had shrunk into a state of crushing self-pity. Our father, who saw our vitality as a sign of good times, paid little attention to us.

I WOULD prefer to forget about the little girl's birth. In her crib, María de Alava was intolerable. When we were forced to look at her, all we saw in her crimson scrawniness were the convulsions of her bad disposition and the oppressiveness of her future form.

My mother, who had been weakened terribly, could only nourish the child at certain times. She was unable to decipher her frame of mind objectively, so she let herself be dragged down by an insipid feeling that even more greatly separated her own being. Her maternal zeal had completed an abundant and alienating cycle which then had begun to extinguish itself, protracting her irritability.

Her life had no meaning or security anymore. Subjected to ongoing transformations, she had run headlong into every pitfall placed in front of her, obligating her body in the process to commit to degenerate experiments. The first and most corrosive trap, of course, was my father himself, who had exploited her – forcing her to perform without considering her own desires or feelings – in vile fashion in order to reaffirm his own self in public.

She used to dream about another life, transcending the opacity of the condition that my father had imposed upon her. She would become doubly horrified when she looked at María de Alava and saw her face expressing hunger.

She felt her breasts and when she squeezed them a stream of milk soaked her cotton shirt. The smell of her own milk nauseated her and she couldn't place her nipple into the little girl's toothless mouth, gaping like a dark, mythic cave.

MY TWIN SISTER and I managed to gain some independence from the narrow family circle. Bewildered by it all, we moved about the house, but our sister's crying, which she used as an instrument to purge the magnitude of her rebellion, followed us everywhere. Wherever we happened to be, her cries were there, so we opted to ignore those exasperating sounds. My twin sister detested her more than I did. Whenever my parents weren't looking, she would climb over her, pin her down, and scratch her.

Once my mother caught her in the act, but her reaction wasn't violent. Even though she had been deprived of her earlier passion, she still maintained a special love for us.

My sister was terrified at being discovered, but when she saw the mist well up in my mother's eyes, she knew that María de Alava had inspired ancient, profound – and destructive – sentiments.

WHEN did a fissure occur inside me? I began to see the world split into two, and the gap in between threatened to swallow me up. Beyond my world, which had fallen apart, was nothing but an abyss.

Consumed by something indescribably fragile, I soon felt as if my body were being severed; I was terrorized by the thought of losing a leg in a race or an arm by just moving it; that my tongue would fall on the floor if I said something. I thought my pupils were going to gyrate uncontrollably outside their orbits and explode into a thousand pieces, leaving me blind.

I was so terrified that I suspended defecating for fear of losing my intestines. So, I had reduced my activity to the point of partial paralysis.

Fear's continual presence had pitted me against a world bent on destroying me and itself. Having become extremely sensitive, I also became the most propitious victim of this potential sacrifice. The unstable movement around me had condensed the whole gamut of perverse emotions threatening to devour me. Since my organism was in the opposition, the only thing I could rely on was the precision of my reasoning. My brain accelerated my anxiety and that, in turn, provoked serious optical disorders and the most unbelievable hearing complications.

Unable to communicate, I sank deeper and deeper into my painful condition and began to fear continually for my disintegrated body. The disproportionate magnitude of my suffering prevented me, a mere five years old, from initiating any kind of real protective action for myself.

At five years of age I felt like the universe was pummeling me with the residue of its deterioration. Everything penetrated me, but I could not reciprocate. Traumatized, I let myself fall toward the abyss, now nothing more than a zone of confusion, crisscrossed with doubts that were in permanent debate. It was an unstable mass playing an eternal, diabolical game.

Shrouded in doubt, even my own existence seemed questionable, or else it was the most tangible proof of an enigmatically vexed world; a world in chaos due to the absence of a guide who would deposit in each being, in every human fetus, peace in their finiteness and pious resignation in their genital appetites. From the moment I perceived the unruly world without institutions or norms, I clashed with my most obscure and critical moment.

My mother, failing in her role of motherhood, was the mass that had trapped me in her flaws, cutting me off from the possibility of falling into my own ruin. With the world severed in two, my only path to reconstruction was my twin sister: being next to her would allow me to achieve wholeness once again.

Getting up was slow and halting at every turn. My sister's energetic body gave me the strength to walk when she let me lean on her shoulder or extend my arm to touch her. Word by word, the validity of her mouth stimulated me. Showing patience with my stumbling and astounded by my premonitions, she took me back to my approximate age.

Little by little, my sister reconstructed my identity, watching me obsessively and transferring her knowledge to me. She forced me to separate my body from my thoughts and to distance myself from the world around me.

By means of the ancestral ritual of game-playing, she introduced me once again to partial stability: 'Don't you understand that a father never veers off track,' she would tell me playing out the role of the indestructible patriarch, while I served as the axis around which she would walk in geometric patterns.

She opted for repetition – that maddening, utilitarian repetition. I even heard her repeatedly in my dreams: 'Don't you understand that a father never veers off track,' words that continued to echo outward in concentric circles.

MY MOTHER'S vice consisted in exposing herself to highly dangerous circumstances in order to reconstruct herself. After failing at every option in the most abnormal fashion, she would collapse into a state of melancholy.

María de Alava grew up surrounded by that world, but she was partially protected by her genetic connection to my dominating father. She had inherited some kind of manly hostility about her that could be deciphered not only from her features and her behavior but also in the way she thought.

Her body was wide and stout. Her stride, marked by a slight bowleggedness, was in unison with the exaggerated, rigid movement of her shoulders. During the first two or three years of her life, these traits consolidated themselves without noticeable alterations. Her likeness to her father, obvious since birth, continued to develop, a process that stimulated his paternal weakness for her. Joyfully aware of this privilege, she was able to avoid her mother, because once again, my mother, now immersed in a serious personal crisis, was living in a fantasy world.

María de Alava would observe us cautiously. Although she spied on us frequently, as if fearing rejection or harassment, she made no attempt to join us. She would play by herself and embellish her own peculiar ceremonies and rituals with mythical animals, like centaurs devouring panthers in ferocious imaginary battles.

At first, we weren't aware of the nature of the beings that she would pit against each other in her narrations, but her guttural jabbering allowed us to discover her secret. My twin sister admired her courage. I thought about the source of her knowledge, and I attributed it to the nature of my mother's dreams, for during the process of conception, she was probably yanked apart by animal impulses. After our initial surprise, her games ceased to amaze or interest us; even her occasional spying on us ceased to annoy us.

María de Alava was a conventional person. She justified everything she did with the same reasoning as our father's.

Taking a personal interest in her, he was the one who took charge of introducing her to the world of language that she finally mastered after some difficulty. He also showed her some of the out-of-the-way places in the house, warning her not to get too close to us and relegating us to alternate spaces.

Unharmed by it all, we were still witnesses to his preference for her and his constant efforts to protect her. His late entrance into paternity was truly puzzling, as if he had felt obliged to duplicate his role in the absence of my mother, who was unable to elude her somnambulism.

None of this affected María de Alava. With herself as her lone audience, she continued playing her delirious zoological games.

At times, when my twin sister's eyes projected homicidal leanings, she would run to my mother who, in those days, was looking for a way to flee from the house. Trembling from the resurgence of sexual frenzy that awoke endless desire in her and anxiety, she was totally given over to planning her escape. Her world was constructed on the fantasy of escape; in fact, a part of her had already abandoned us. She held onto her charm though: she always did what she was asked, but a close look at her revealed her gestures and movements as purely mechanical. She didn't see or look at anything beyond her own images and voices.

OUR TREKS to the outside world were astounding. The city, taciturnly benevolent, awoke all kinds of desires and activated fantasies we inherited from my mother. Among the crowded citizenry populating the streets, we could feel the libidinous traffic that consolidated crime and selling. The beautiful, bare torsos of the young sudaca boys were like living sculptures walking down the sidewalks. During our brief outings, our eyes absorbed a seemingly vast orgy. My twin sister was dazzled by the sight of male musculature and her dry lips revealed her thoughts. One could perceive in her heavy-lidded eyes a precocious lasciviousness.

Torn pants that allowed her to catch a glimpse of a leg would leave her with a mysteriously penetrating and primeval look on her face. I was seeing all that through her eyes until I lowered mine; the potent images made me blush.

Those curious, opulent sudaca men seemed as if they were about to explode in the fervor of the city. My sister and I would dream about losing ourselves in those back streets and tragically sacrificing our youthful innocence.

AT SCHOOL, we experienced humiliation. It took a while for us to put aside our previous ordeals and to concentrate on learning. We couldn't deal with the multitude of impossible, gaunt beings who populated the classrooms. Our circumspection and my sister's craftiness provoked envy on the part of the other children who never ceased to attack us. My twin sister was shocked by the vulgarity of the place and detested being confused with the rest of the group. She sought ways to stand above them, either by using my mother's perfumes or by using keen insight to point out defects in the others.

We had no trouble learning the different school subjects; we easily channeled our intelligence, which irritated the other children even more because they had to struggle to learn simple information and uncomplicated graphs.

My sister liked to boast about her achievements. She would make fun of the others by inventing denigrating nicknames that quickly spread throughout the school.

Her way of expending energy was too much for me. Exhausted by the presence of so many sudaca bodies and frightened by the mundane pandemonium of the children, my ambivalence drained me, putting me to sleep anywhere. My complexion became so sallow and pale that my facial features seemed to recede. My twin sister would pinch my cheeks to bring back the color but the reddening effect would disappear in an instant.

As I dozed off, fragments of diverse stories filled with screaming, and bloodied thighs, would coalesce in my dreams. The color red, the true protagonist of those visions, gushed forth thickly with images of death. Once again, something was suffocating my organism but, at the same time, it was alerting my brain to begin to generate defense mechanisms.

To expend as little effort as possible was something out of my reach. I was unable to concentrate, so the ease with which I had been learning became difficult.

Once again my mother had to confront my new sickness. Proceeding in accord with her own intuitions, she fed me a mixture of bitter herbs that slowly brought back my health and gave me the strength to face the public sphere.

During that time, my twin sister developed banal, irritating habits. In order to exercise every last bit of my authority over her, I had to humiliate and scorn her talents. Since she was extremely vulnerable, she began, once again, to elaborate complex and profound gestures that were the key to our mutual understanding.

Her temporary change in behavior was meant to exclude me, enabling her to strike out on her own in search of other lasting affection.

ABRUPTLY, I became disinterested in my mother's mythological reincarnations. Her presence became a part of the household activities to the point that she was practically transformed into another simple object, there to serve the needs of the others. In fact, I came to understand that to think about her for more than a second made me feel ashamed.

Occasionally, she would attempt to envelop me in exaggerated demonstrations of affection that I would reject outright. The game amused my mother and she would smile ironically, but I would always avoid her by disappearing.

Her constant ironies kept me at a distance most of the time because I didn't know how to respond to her or how to fight back. Nearing eleven years, I refused to let her bathe me, especially when I would see her grinning as she poured warm water over my naked body. In a way, I was beginning to free myself from all personal contact, allowing her to help me only at times of maximum disinterestedness. She didn't oppose my quiet and decisive efforts to establish detachment. Sensitive to my behavior, she immediately understood the meaning of what I was doing and she released me with her indifference.

The only thing that seemed to annoy her was the close bond my twin sister and I had developed. She contrived to separate us, but my sister undermined her efforts with obsessive pleas. She tried to push my two sisters together but neither one of them showed any liking for the other; in fact, they would come to blows for any reason and usually María de Alava was the one who suffered the most.

I couldn't stand all that commotion, so I would cover my ears trying to avoid going crazy. If they got close to each other, I would tense up, in anticipation of those unbearable confrontations that I knew so well. Sometimes I was the pretext for their fighting. If I asked María de Alava a simple question, my twin sister would unleash her wrath on her, ready to pounce. Afterward she would run away, leaving her sister crying hysterically and violently upset.

Frankly, I was alarmed by the family quarreling. No one was thinking logically, for vanity and jealousy had taken over. Like my mother, I yearned to abandon the house and to look for a homogeneous masculine paradise on the outside.

MY FATHER, while distant, treated me decently. His only eccentricity was to go out occasionally to buy me clothes. His eyes would twinkle when he examined them, as he demonstrated his wide knowledge of different grades of cloth. He would gently rub the cloth between his fingers and accurately describe its quality and durability. Silk shirts were his preference. I shared the same propensity for silk, and it would send chills down my spine when it touched my skin. My father would take hours to make a choice. He would spread out two or three shirts on the display counter, comparing and examining their quality and the clarity of their colors. The pleats delighted him and he would run his fingertips over the surface of the cloth as if he were intimately caressing someone, quivering with implacable impotency.

During those moments of ecstasy, I was nonexistent. When he was about to decide, he ordered me to give the final word. But it was then that I could see a sense of disappointment in his eyes, as if my body had somehow diminished the quality of the cloth or my face had defiled the splendor of its beauty.

WHEN I turned twelve years old, I had my first sexual encounter. Transmuted by the ancestral force of passion, I was on the verge of consummating the act, but I didn't know then if I was being liberated to experience glory or to experience punishment, for all I wanted was to go further – I had to go much further – until I could fuse hesitation with acceleration, disorder with precision, in the sacred flesh.

It happened on a street. The sky was darkened with clouds. I was walking attentively along a narrow street when I sensed that someone was following me. My heart began to pound, yearning for the secret pleasure that emerged from some part of my brain.

I soon realized that I was not the one being followed, but the one following someone else, someone slender, walking unhurriedly, and seeming to glide along in an affected manner. The equivocal situation made me fear that I was hallucinating, but the sound of the steps, the crisp air, and the uneven sidewalk confirmed that I was deeply immersed in a real situation.

I was astonished to realize that not only was I following an unknown person but also I didn't know why I was doing it. Inexplicably, and in some crucial way, however, that moment pulled me away from the world I knew and pushed me into another in which that hieroglyphic person would make similarity and difference fade into one another.

At one particular moment I lost sight of the figure. Dejected and vexed by inertia, I began to double back, thinking nostalgically about my loss. I felt deprived of some absolute presence, more fundamental than my parents and more mysterious than the sum of my fluctuations.

Sadly, I started back. Of the four roads from which I could

choose, each one was as equally possible as it was a mistake. I quickly realized that not only had I lost someone but also, in the search, I had become lost myself.

It would have been absurd to wager on which way I should return. One of those roads would take me home, but if I were to choose the wrong one, it would take me three times as long to get back. It seemed as if I were being punished for letting myself be guided by my impulses. Soon it was going to get dark and the city would become even more dangerous. I had been warned about it so many times that now it seemed like a dream to be exposed to it, just on the edge of twilight and shielded by anonymous, conventional dwellings.

Some curious faces observed me while I stood there, stubborn and rigid, trying to decide which way to go. Becoming desperate, I tried to reconstruct my original route, but each possibility seemed equally valid to me. As I got cold, I became more anxious, so I made a random choice. I had no memories or assumptions that would have convinced me that I should have headed south.

I was facing a long and lonely walk, intensified by fear every step of the way. There was nothing to distract me, except the darkness that was overtaking the sky ever so quickly.

Suddenly, when my miserable condition was too much for me to bear, I saw that same figure standing nearby. I froze, overwhelmed by irrepressible desire. Without thinking, I walked through the darkness, guided only by the scent of another person's skin near me. I stopped.

I felt myself being pushed up against the stone wall, breathing in unison with the figure that was stroking me. Expert, soft hands ran all over my body and fingers pushed against me in order to remove my clothing. In that public exchange, those hands that traversed my body back and forth found their way to the most stimulated part of me.

Unable to feel the stone wall jabbing at my back anymore, I sought a deeper reality once those caresses had prepared me for that moment. Feeling totally outside my body, I tried to touch the other person, but a pair of hands stopped me.

As if in apology, our mouths became fused with the passion of our saliva. My tongue became a sword, seeking not only to wound my rival but also to lick my ally.

Our mouths witnessed a combat of shifting liquids that became desperately and painfully prolonged. My breathing became nasally vulgar as the undulations, domination, and pricking left me out of breath. Unable to continue, I decided to consummate the act, but the figure fled, leaving me stinging against the stone wall.

Then the pain began. A sharp, genital pain, provoked by vigorous and demanding desire. Alone and shameless, I resigned myself to the personal glory that I had assiduously attained for the first time. Satisfaction was measured by the curve of desire and the dimension of abandonment. When the violence of the stones returned, I knew it was over.

The hours it took me to get home were agonizing, for I cursed and cursed the whole way, trying to destroy my sexual vitality. I saw myself as an outcast, I was unworthy of living with my family, and I felt as if my mind and body had been condensed into all the encrusted afflictions of the world.

At intervals, strong surges of well-being helped return me to a state of moderation, reducing the denigrated feeling I had about myself. The acursed sermon of reason incessantly accused me of a perfidious crime whose fine was permanent shame and horror.

I promised to make all kinds of sacrifices, even castration, in order to alleviate that burden; yet something had become hopelessly perverted in me and, deep inside, I had exposed myself to a cynical yet honest life.

I suffered intensely for several days but, little by little, even though I was feeling much anxiety, I concentrated on elucidating exactly what happened in that meeting on the street.

I couldn't determine who or what seduced me that evening. Despite continually reconstructing that encounter I could never ascertain anything with any proof, even though I know I encountered youthful plenitude in the flesh of a young female beggar or a young male vagabond who, as night approached, performed a charitable act for me.

MY TWIN SISTER figured out immediately what had happened. At first, I would stubbornly deny what I had categorized as her delirious suppositions. Then, when she continued to pressure me, I used the silent treatment, which irritated her, in order to drive her away. There was nothing I could do to stop her, and she even began offering me presents to entice me to describe the incident in detail.

She offered me just about everything she possessed, even those things she prized the most and with which she spent all of her time playing. When I finally gave in, it wasn't because I was tempted by her offers but because I had the urgent need to interpret the events of that evening.

At first I stuttered and felt embarrassed, but then the words began to flow in extraordinarily precise fashion, stimulated by my sister's expression of amazement that, in turn, stimulated me to be even more bold. The expression on her face oscillated between pale comprehension and the blushing guilt of eroticism.

Even though I was nourishing her with experiences unknown to her, the depth of her envy could be seen in her twitching, unsustainable smile. I wasn't interested in placating her feelings because she had returned again and again to the compulsive reiteration of the past, as if the impact of the details could evoke the physical ardor of my experiences.

I acknowledge that I wasn't cognizant of the real effect that the incident had on my sister's consciousness because I was performing according to my own compulsions and weaknesses. Not long afterward, fever and disease debilitated her almost to the point of death.

I hardly slept during that period. Delirious with fever, she would say my name frequently and, worse yet, narrate fragments of the episode I had told her. My parents could not understand everything she was saying, yet they did sense its perverse nature, impossible for a twelve-year-old girl to know about. They harbored repudiation and astonishment which were combined with the pain of their next potential loss. I confess that I felt relieved when they couldn't put two and two together, but the terror I experienced over my sister's imminent parting intensified.

It was impossible for me to conceive of life without my sister. A part of me ended in her, perhaps the most stable and permanent part.

I stayed by her side night and day. Pustules took over her body, preventing her from drinking, seeing, or moving. Her slender form – now a flimsy skeleton – had turned yellowish. She was covered with eruptions that her tiny hands scratched raw, leaving the sheets – they had to be changed several times a day – stained with blood and pus. My mother was told that she would have to let the disease run its course and everything depended on the stamina of my sister's body.

With rumors that death was not long in coming, chaos reigned in the house. Gossip seemed to scale the walls and watch us through the windows. But I wouldn't be intimidated. I knew that somehow I was immune because my sister had invoked evil in order to free her own desires. In fact, she had invoked death in order to punish me and herself. I also knew, albeit confusedly, that a possible cure for her depended on me, although I didn't know how to achieve it.

During the hours my parents slept, I would sit on the edge of her bed and hope for some sign of hope from the inner depths of her body.

She would sit up in pain from time to time and repeat bits and pieces of the incident that I, of course, wanted to forget. Without a doubt, my twin sister was succumbing to death, becoming weaker by the moment, her life hanging in the balance.

I wasn't going to let her desert me. I was disposed to do anything, I was desperate to restore her arrogant resistance to the outside world. I concentrated on reviewing our past, searching for something that might explain her impending demise. After eliminating the majority of the feelings that were manifest in her, one aspect remained intact: the one obsession controlling her was the basis of her crisis.

Even as I realized this, I was unable to determine the exact cause of what had set into motion the obsessive affliction that I had decided I was ready to attempt to heal. I became quite obsessed by it, but it seemed natural to me because I was facing the imminence of her death.

Fearing there was no solution, I felt as if my head were about to explode: I was convinced that I was committing fratricide.

Thinking again, I figured out there was a common thread between the two of us and, occupying the part that corresponded to her, I interrogated myself about what might constitute a rupture. A voice of truth clarified everything for me. Like an ancient, experienced healer, I dragged myself over to her bed that reeked of pestilence and suffering and I began to talk to her with the love of one sick person to another, telling her I believed that the other person – he or she – who assaulted me in that narrow street will always be she, that I knew exactly what was happening, that she was there, it was she, we were there, us, together. I rested my hand on her neck, now shriveled from the infection, in order to make her understand that I wasn't afraid of her, but her rigid body still continued to dominate me.

The reality of my words lifted the veil that she anxiously tried to maintain intact. Sobbing, I dropped my head to her chest. Having understood, she put her hand on my head.

Then came improvement. It took me a while to be able to look at her face to face; it seemed as though something evil had come between us and we were abruptly condemned to the desolate absence of fantasy.

MY MOTHER had a serious conversation with my sister. Probing her habits, she placed her within her reality and determined her sense of relationship to her surroundings. Warning her about the effect her delirious mumbling had on my parents, I gave her the strength to survive the encounter.

She spoke in a confessional tone about the turbulent dreams that had tormented her. One could tell that a dreamlike delirium had consumed her physically like never before. My mother thought she understood; after that, however, she totally isolated María de Alava from us.

One could feel tension everywhere. My sister's demure behavior annoyed us. She didn't play with my mother's perfumes anymore, and she stopped demonstrating her loving attributes.

I refused to participate in her farce. Her hostile attitude toward my mother became all too obvious. Inevitably, I could see that my mother was deeply jealous of my sister and she would conceal her feelings by adopting a harsh, peculiar moral stance. My sister was being punished, not for what she was doing but for what she was – a child who grew up tormenting her mother.

I feared revenge. I could perceive that an aging woman was

capable of anything in order to conceal getting old. It was necessary to praise my sister, so I would observe her performances. I told her what I disliked the most: that her immutable adolescent smile was so disconnected from her gaze, her walk, her words.

As I told my sister about her childish smile, my mother's eyes became veiled in tears. To my chagrin, I could see how once again she continued to be shackled by the evil appetites entombed in her mind as deeply as ever.

I advised my sister to keep her distance from my mother. I couldn't accept her being sacrificed by another woman's age. We guardedly began going out again. Shielded by the impossible, we endured the staring that seemed to judge us from every corner of the house.

OH! THE TERROR and the hounding of blood! I remember when my sister bled for the first time: almost thirteen years old, she embarked on a separate journey of uneasiness that I would never experience. Frightened and anxious about the phenomenon awaiting her, she had tried to talk to me about it before. I refused to listen to her, much less comment on something that seemed dirty and personal.

But the day arrived when my sister discovered blood between her legs and she reacted as if someone had slapped her in the face. I could see that she had turned terribly pale as she held her lower abdomen in her hands, still reeling from the astonishment. As tears ran down her cheeks, she didn't want to accept her infertility.

As I stared at her, I could tell that was the last time she would look like a harmless child, now about to be disfigured. I didn't know how to console her, nor did I want to; something definitive came between us. She paid the price of her sex and proved her commonality with that affiliation. I was moved by her genetic meekness, as if our budding unity signified nothing or, at least, nothing important.

I was unable to conceal my feelings. My sister felt guilty and innocent at the same time, and I could see she harbored other feelings of condemnation that were capable of eroding even more the sign of our alliance.

A burst of blood paralyzed us. Terrified, I realized that my nose was bleeding profusely. I pulled my hand away from my face; it was dripping with blood, and my shirt was splattered with red spots. We looked at each other without saying anything; any feelings of pride disappeared immediately. The intimate, oppressive, and absolute link between us had been miraculously reestablished.

I should confess that a cold, wet cloth immediately stopped the bleeding, but it didn't eliminate the potential meaning of something more profound.

Without really knowing whether this act was an attempt to fuse myself with her or, to the contrary, I was making her responsible for unleashing my blood, we intuitively pulled away from each other – fearful of establishing the habit of transfusions.

As long as I can remember, we never discussed the incident again. My sister's cycles came and went in silent seclusion. Pale and emaciated, she would withdraw from me knowing that her condition disgusted me.

When she finally returned to her natural beauty, we always became talkative, describing the onslaught of men and women lunging at us along the narrow streets.

DESIRE. The explicit emotion of desire. The irregular palpitations of an open, infected wound. Supply and demand became concentrated in my body, moving back and forth between debasement and exaltation. Shielded by the serenity of the night, I was overtaken by insomnia and saw myself as a naked woman in a barren field, feeling the cosmic magnitude of giving birth.

The censurable operation of my hand responded to the clamoring of my flesh and invalidated the modesty that the most intangible part of my being, now violated, had sought to confirm.

As vital as food, my desire was generated – against my will – out of death. In the open battle of body against mind, I had lost any cognizance of my own being.

The assault could occur at any moment; hence, I feared being alone, like one fears the intensity of darkness as a child. I understood that this primitive fear was only a prelude to the impending reckless battle between body and mind.

There's nothing more threatening than the rite with which the body enjoys itself; and nothing more humiliating than the lifeless, exhausted body burdened with sensual images that reappear abundantly and forcefully.

My walks through the streets resembled a collection of visions that, afterward when I was alone, I would reconstruct according to my whims. The dissolution of my integrity – now subservient to the petitions of my stubbornly active and clandestine cellular tissues – seemed hard to believe.

I had to become accustomed to my body, just as I had to get used to all the irregularities in my life, such as the accumulation of the anger of the victim destined not to share secrets, to show off, or to revel in perversion.

MY SISTER was consumed by silk and glitter. Her thirteen-year-old body exploded out of infancy and her figure foretold the advent of puberty. Different periods were distinguished by the dresses she would improvise for me. Since she had no style, I was her mentor and audience. I thought purple suited her best. She would paint her cheeks that color and it would ooze down to her lips. Sometimes I preferred red and, if I was feeling calm, I would smear soft rose hues on her.

Attempting desperately to create her own style, her ardent performance would enslave me at her side for hours on end, but I attempted to please her. The makeup made her look absurd and the dresses she put on would do nothing to make her hips and breasts stand out; instead she looked skinny. She only looked attractive when she tried on something that corresponded to her age.

On those occasions, her true age would be threatened, for the ensuing years seemed to pass through her body in a savagely carnal and alluring way. But she resisted, influenced by her fantasy of women who were exacting and univocal.

Her vanity grew like the winter darkness. Living inside herself and only for herself, she used the pupils of my eyes to mirror herself, to explain herself, to savor herself.

I knew that she was thwarting her own desires. I would be present for that string of painful acts in which she would repudiate herself in order to suspend the disturbing present. Agitated and suffering, by nightfall she would be worn out and her pale face would give in to the fatigue of her tired body.

Nevertheless, one day in the middle of one of her outbursts she told me that she was unable to contain herself any longer. Aware of the deep pain that she was going to cause me, she told me everything: about armies of boys and girls dwelling in her mind, about the sudaca beggars who pursued her, trying to slash her to pieces.

She wanted to leave the house and dance the world away until she fell down dead. For her, every passing minute meant more lost time. Inside the house, she was condemned to live a cloistered life, whereas outside those confining walls, the entire world was enjoying itself. It was like an eternal party, and I was her guard, her most fierce jailer. She spoke to me with hatred in her eyes – hatred that was icy cold.

Soon she succumbed to hysteria and accused me of the most perverse intentions. She insisted that I was playing with her mind in order to drive her insane. It was torture. Even as I stood there observing her, I almost couldn't believe that she was truly saying those things.

She seemed like a small evil spirit and, losing my self-control, I countered with my own accusations. Also assailed by hysteria, I denounced her feminine pathos and her ridiculous relationship to the world around her. Her role in the party of the universe, I said, would be the most despicable of all, for without me she had no life, without me she couldn't even become a peasant. I ridiculed not only her skimpy figure but also her inability to think because she was always shrouded in the mediocrity of her own cunning.

Yelping like a puppy, she leaped on me and started hitting me. I responded by hitting back. Reacting like a husband who had just learned that his wife was copulating with every Tom, Dick, and Harry, I returned the attack, seeking revenge for the burden of her that I had supported since the second day of my life. By striking her, I was also striking myself.

I was, in truth, experiencing the privilege of violence, for I felt capable of committing a crime – one that would allow me to bring this conflict to an end.

As she sprawled on the floor, I kept hitting and kicking her. All of a sudden she stopped moaning and the silence not only surprised me but also brought me back to my senses. Puzzled by my behavior, I looked at her with more surprise than regret. I couldn't believe I was capable of such rage, so I just stared at her, searching for the reason of my fury. There she was, curled up into a tiny ball; her eyes seemed even more serene and the convulsions in her face had disappeared. Despite the red streaks on her cheeks, arms, and legs, she had recovered her normal beauty.

She seemed to be smiling but I thought it was an optical illusion, so I took a second look: there was a definite smile on her mouth.

We heard our mother's voice at the doorway. From the expression on her face, we could tell she had witnessed the entire incident. After my sister got to her feet, we confronted her together. I was too embarrassed to invent some excuse. Frankly, it wasn't necessary because my mother, upon entering the room, leaned against the wall and hid her face in her hands.

THE BOYS were continually coming over, trying to woo my sister. Like peacocks, they would strut and pose with affectation. Hoping to make me an accomplice to their desires, they would flatter me by proposing absurd tests of rivalry that, in turn, meant letting them come over to our house. There was one among them who seemed to be devastated by the passion he felt for her; tall and muscular, his behavior changed radically. Before he had met my sister, he was arrogant, aggressive, and made fun of people; then he became so alarmingly vulnerable that people began to pity him.

His bashfulness around my sister, which seemed so feminine to me, didn't correspond to his masculine side that betrayed his desire for quick possession. He was like an open book: anyone could interpret the nocturnal and diurnal fantasies gushing from his sweaty, trembling hands and his body that swelled significantly and stiffly when he was around her.

Then he wanted to demonstrate his exemplary side, but his attempts failed utterly; in their place, he substituted a pathetic, paternal kindness that he thought would save his life. And he was ready to give his life away in order to procure part of hers.

The boy was overcome with passion; his beauty was becoming so pristine that his movements had become equally exquisite. On the one hand, he looked like the product of prolonged sentimental neglect; on the other hand, one might think that he had been pampered to extremes and, for the first time in his life, he wanted to reciprocate.

The inexorable and insecure masculine world knocked him off the pedestal assigned to him. Everyone teased him and called him all kinds of silly nicknames pertaining to little girls.

Curiously, none of that bothered him; on the contrary, he seemed to take pleasure in the humiliation, now widespread and making his sacrifice almost mystical. Without flinching, he welcomed the attacks, as if his brutal marginalization were the price he had to pay in order to achieve his desires.

My sister's vanity grew like a new sun in the universe, vibrating between rejection and attraction. The boy, desirous of greater sacrifices and reciprocal gestures of love, would take each new schism as a sign of honor. Since I never stopped observing her, I could tell how he was getting inside her mind from a degrading but not any less significant position.

Of course, my sister couldn't understand the enormous difference that existed between them and how that gave him a strategic advantage. The boy, feeling threatened by her growing beauty, was using her in his headlong rush into sin.

He had decided to abdicate, resigning himself to the domination of my sister and, thus, freeing himself from his own supremacy. In order for seduction to triumph over the masculine model, now clearly outmoded, failure and panic were next.

I could see that my sister was about to fall for it. She could only be trapped by someone who would evasively imitate her own gender and caste, by whomever was capable of sharing and imputing to her his diminished and dangerous place.

While I was overwhelmed by his sacrifice, I could understand how he had plumbed the depths of the confusing feminine mind, learning how it appreciated change but was devoted to permanence. Seeking change could exact a high price in women and become more enslaving and long-lasting than the archetype itself.

He had learned to keep his distance from me. Indifferent, I bore no animosity toward him. And our house didn't seem to constitute an obsession for him either, but he made his shrewdness evident in the classroom and in the street.

My eyes knew no truce and I was driven by my mania for observation. I would spend hours deciphering events and situations. In privileged moments, I attained such high levels of knowledge that I feared I would acquire the capability of deciphering secret hieroglyphics. There was nothing that interested me less, but it seemed as though the mystery simply appeared before me offering itself like a starved woman.

Even though my mind kept on unraveling the threads of human conduct, I didn't want to examine my own behavior or recognize my anguish. Unintentionally, he helped me find myself. During this whole time, my obvious malaise had possessed me, crushing me with anxiety.

I was unable to accept affection that they shared, so I found myself not only excluded but miserable. I almost felt the same way they did; in fact, my affection resonated more intensely than theirs but, nevertheless, nothing was entirely mine except the surplus of someone else's feelings. Like a parasite, I would negate my self-esteem.

I suspected that the whole thing was nothing more than one of my sister's narcissistic maneuvers, for which jealousy had become the motivating force of love. My twin sister didn't trust my affection, so she created obstacles and provided painful evidence to prove it. Feigning indifference, I wanted to let them strike up an alliance between themselves. In that way, I would be completely triumphant, but it was necessary to hold back my anxiety because my precarious state needed mending quickly.

Jealousy overtook hatred, hatred overtook abandonment, and animosity seemed to be the lookout from which the cataclysm of my mind could be detected. With each day of torment came the fear of having to face the next one. I had exhausted my strength, so I decided to take the offensive in order to crush my twin sister and to let it be known that she had played her last game with me.

Those two amalgamated forms – clasped together in an embrace or locked in battle in the tepid waters – began to appear in my dreams again. I was going to have to respond to those voracious images and I prepared myself to confront her like a lover on a first date.

I paid no attention to myself, I only sought harmony. Graceful like a panther and sensual like an oriental courtier, I erased the boy from her mind.

I availed myself of an attractive but insignificant sudaca girl who, without understanding what I was doing, yielded to my request. Slowly and softly, my fingers roamed far and wide while my extraordinarily sagacious muscles responded perfectly.

There was no ending, nothing consummated, only the supremacy of the stone wall that reflected the last rays of the afternoon sun. Nevertheless, my sister felt cold and trembled as if half the night had enveloped her.

MARÍA DE ALAVA continued to remain close to my father because that relationship gave her security and even changed her behavior. She would walk around the house as if she were inspecting her own dominions. Her maneuverability was surprising and she demonstrated how well she could control her body. Like an expert juggler, she was in perfect harmony with the things around her, taking advantage of them for her own benefit. Her stocky – even virile – build seemed to contradict her tight-rope walker's balance.

I was amused to watch her play games and to perform with such solemnity. She would play as if she were on the edge of an abyss or avoiding a wall of roaring flames. She would evade a dangerous panther perched high up on a rock, survive an attack, and then conquer it.

Most of the time, she would pretend she was immersed in water harboring devilish aquatic creatures that were trying to devour her, but she would always escape to the surface of the breaking waves and be saved.

The ocean that was unfamiliar to us seemed to obsess her. Ships ferried her directly to catastrophe. She would either sink with shipwrecked vessels that had been damaged by the storms or flee from sturdy ships carrying monsters that wanted to sacrifice her. The scenes she created were perfect, right down to feigning the scratches and scrapes on her body as she writhed on the beach.

Her games would always end the same way: hugging her in his arms, the figure of my father would carry her to safety. She would pretend he was some hero – a sailor, a watchman, a captain, a gladiator – which he might well have been because the way he was dressed didn't match her imagination. His hair, gestures, and behavior, which she would describe in detail, corresponded exactly to the way he was.

Clearly, María de Alava was acting out stories contrived by my father. His masterwork dealt with the theme of death fraught with significant – almost suicidal – tension. Invariably, death would be subdued only to appear again in another lively skit. My younger sister was the bearer of death that my father had sought, reducing her necessarily to two opposing poles: success or failure, goodness or badness, life or death. It was in this very conventional impoverished state that my father had taken root in her so profoundly. Only on certain occasions did he display different traits that coincided with his confrontation with the family female nucleus.

As for his relationship with my mother or my twin sister, it was necessary for him to invent cautious strategies because they had imposed a series of obstacles for him to expedite his demands.

My mother would torment my younger sister at mealtime by referring to her pudgy body. Gesticulating hysterically, she blamed her excessive appetite, saying that it threatened to give shape to a ridiculous body that would eventually embarrass the family.

My sister would never contradict her: she simply tried very hard to reduce her intake, knowing that the root of her problem was not the amount of food she ate but her body type.

However, the majority of the conflicts involved my twin sister who would accuse her younger sibling, in front of my mother, of tormenting her, stealing, and lying. Punishment ensued but my father would always intercede and rescue her.

Naturally, my sister was partially to blame for the hostility between them. Her complacency was, no doubt, a heightened form of aggression; in addition, in no situation did she ever show affection.

The limits of her familial affections were condensed to her relationship with me. Although she didn't grant me the status of hero, she placed me in a superior position, making physical intimacy necessary. Knowing I was alone, she would invade the recesses of my room and dance for me.

Dancing – a strangely timeless ritual complete with body contortions – was another one of her aptitudes. Her passion for dancing unfolded with the beauty of youthful immortality. Close and distant, grieving and vivacious, her body would dance the history of the world; her face danced the bonfires of her feet, and she seemed to expel her thoughts so they would dance and satiate their contents.

Few times have I seen a similar spectacle performed according to the plenitude of my desires. Certain that we were alone, I would dance with her, being led and stimulated by her, and my body would give itself up to my most exquisite perceptions and dreams. While seemingly sensual, I had gone beyond sensuality itself; I felt unreal, as if I were carrying the reality of the human race inside me.

We sought to define the dimensions of time and its design that my younger sister had understood from the infinity of her ten years. That's why I could imitate her, read her thoughts, and give her a simile. It concerned life, not death; or life despite death, undulating inside us like a tribute to our roots, our heroes, and our beggars: a celebration of our painful human sorrows and of the uncertainty of our future.

It was a sacred dance that related directly to the earth; the dance embodied it, becoming possible only through an earth that contained the perfection of our feet, enabling our yearning bodies to entwine the universe and to remake it.

Without shunning human nature, our bodies exhibited hatred and envy, lust and corruption, with the same emphasis as the amazement of the species of giving birth. Observing ourselves for our capacity to exist, we would disintegrate and be reborn again, now distant from and outside the world of words, managing to live in a time unfamiliar to time.

That was our secret. After we had finished the dance, María de Alava would leave the room closing the door behind her. Stretched out on the floor, I let the limbs of my body go limp. Once my subconscious took over, the dance began to repeat itself, depositing its magnificent evanescence in the deepest hollows of my bones.

MY FATHER'S anger would explode like the final dissipation of a spent star. He shouted that contradicting his authority was the same as violently opposing our family, all of which caused us much anxiety – especially when we learned that hatred had brought my parents together. It wasn't necessary for us to know the reasons why they were always arguing or who had caused the quarrel: the pounding on the furniture and my mother's hysterical wailing – calling for his death as she prayed for her own death – were already frightening enough.

Both of them said the worst things to each other, hurting each other as if the words themselves possessed some definitive power and physical force. Sometimes it would seem as if their fighting would finally reach a stalemate, but all of sudden they would violently go at each other again, their voices triggering more animosity. The family fell to pieces, it was a sham. We judged it to be a hostile marriage, its perpetual union now exhausted, enslaving them to their filial bonds.

Unable to explain their resentment, and feeling caged within the catastrophic circumstances of the family, they would accuse each other of destroying each other's lives. Although my mother was the most accurate and pitiless, she would finally acquiesce to the wishes of my father, who invariably would announce his intentions to leave. My mother would see herself disgraced by defeat and abandonment and imagine multitudes of women carrying their sobbing children over mountains and through swamps; she pictured swarms of hungry orphans subjected to the flesh trade; and she would visualize herself as a rheumatic, crazy old lady, awaiting death in a nursing home on the outskirts of the city. She presumed that her mature body, now single, might succumb to the excesses of voyeuristic palpations through the windows of her room.

My mother would always capitulate to him because she thought that my father, once he was out of the house, would search for happiness through amorous adventures, replete with women who would satisfy him for free; yes, this was my father, seeking ecstasy and making a mockery of what the family was supposed to be. Her only goal was to attempt to recover the cyclical tragedy of her own humiliation.

Even at that, my mother was forever seeking confrontation and making a game out of her supposed misfortune. She seemed to be waiting for her final collapse and the destruction of the family, but at the moment of truth she would fall back and suppress temptation.

My father considered this disruption a natural part of life. He thought it was useful for maintaining balance and for reminding us of the range of his authority. He never seriously considered leaving home; in fact, the very thought was unbearable because, beyond the confines of our house, he was insecure. The oppression he would feel from the houses in the city triggered a state of infantile helplessness, which, in turn, forced him to relive his own passage into adulthood.

But in my mother's presence, he was able to banish his fears by conforming to his genetic purpose; the disputes, therefore, were fundamental to him because in that way he could satisfy – uninjured and triumphantly – his warlike drives.

Later on, I was able to grasp the origins of the game between them. For a long time my frail heart had absorbed the devastating effects of the paternal figure that punished his flock.

WHEN I was thirteen years old, I was brutally attacked by a mob of angry young sudacas. I had been walking along a jetty where I would spend hours quietly observing the waves. Despite their presence throughout the city, I took notice of the sudacas off in the distance; on this occasion the group moving in my direction made me uneasy. I decided to turn back and avoid the group by going up a side street, but I immediately felt embarrassed by my cowardice.

It was cloudy and cold that afternoon. I tried to disappear inside my clothes. As they got closer, I could see that their facial expressions all looked alike.

For a fleeting second, I thought their profiles recalled the architecture of the city, leaving passersby disorientated and confused but realizing how differences mimicked each other. Something similar could be seen in the faces of those young people; their lower-class roots gave them a singular unity which could be observed in their distinct, individual movements. The effectiveness of those movements, all precisely accentuated and extremely provocative, was common to all of them.

As they walked past me, I thought I had become alarmed needlessly, but suddenly one of them grabbed me. Immobilized, I found myself surrounded by an indeterminate number of shadowy forms. They began to take jabs at me. I was so frightened that I thought I was experiencing a nightmare. The street was deserted, so I knew no one would come to my rescue; having already panicked, I couldn't yell or escape, either.

The mob was laughing and speaking a meaningless dialect. They pushed me against a wall and began to throw punches. I managed to ward them off, but my body rocked and swayed grotesquely, inciting them to laugh even more. Knowing fully well that I was making the worst move of my life, I lunged at the leader.

I kicked him hard, which took him by surprise; then I managed to free myself and began jabbing wildly at him. The group reacted immediately and I was thrown to the ground. Pain overwhelmed me. The beating was unrelenting: I couldn't feel my body anymore. The impartiality of the pain between my head and my stomach reached all the way to the bottom of my feet; I didn't even feel the blood flowing from the gash on my jaw.

Inside my brain, however, my anger continued to grow. Somehow I managed to stand up and look directly at the guy I had hit earlier. Staggering, I tried to reach him while the others closed in around me. Each step I took was excruciatingly difficult. Totally dazed, I could only see their figures bobbing back and forth. I was possessed by one single idea: continue forward. I raised my arm in order to attack, but I tripped and fell. Once again I managed to pull myself up, this time clutching the guy's leg; he looked down at me. Slowly, desperately, I tried to stand up, retaining his silhouette in my eyes, but they went cloudy. Half-blind, I sagged against his rigid, motionless body.

I had no strength left and I collapsed once again, falling headlong into the silent darkness of nothingness.

I learned afterward that they had left me in front of my house, propped up against the front door. That evening I felt the first bolt of pain traverse my jaw, where I had a deep, open wound. I witnessed the formation of my first scar that took its place on the lower side of my face.

VIOLENCE erupted in the middle of the night. My twin sister burst into my room while I was asleep and kept shaking me until I woke up. The dim light gave her the glow of a vision, but there was her beautiful barefoot shadow looking straight at me.

We have to talk, she said, and we have to talk openly. We need to express our emotions, which we haven't done before. She said we had to squeeze from our muteness all that had separated us and about which we were completely innocent.

She explained that her silence had been imposed on her by me because I had ordered her mind to follow habits that had finally consumed her.

Her words made an impact on me. I got up and sat next to her. I was prepared to tell her everything, for I had been overcome by the urgency to talk. I was distracted by the movement of her hands; despite the faint light, I could see that the nails of her slender fingers were black. I looked at her feet; they were also encrusted with dry, dark dirt.

My twin sister had gone outside where something or someone had called her attention. I could just see her flying out the door of her room; I could also imagine her body tumbling into the dirt in the garden, pushed down by an unquestionably masculine figure.

Instantly, I re-created the grimly tempestuous scene. In that unending split second, I considered trying to escape or throwing her out of my room. But I took her right hand and scraped at the dirt that clung tenaciously to her fingernails. At first my sister, who was nervous, tried to pull away, but then, flashing that familiar smile that had already occasioned much grief, she let me continue.

I wanted to – I had to – think of a way to break away from her. She wanted to drag me down to the point of suicidal alienation and, in the end, donate my corpse. I felt as if I were being nibbled at by armies of ants that marched all over my body; I also sensed misfortune was upon me.

I removed the last particle of dirt from the nail of her little finger and only then did I look into her eyes. She stood up, driven by sensuality, and struggled to remove her nightshirt. I just stared at the floor, disapprovingly. The ring of distant church bells startled me. Dawn was upon us and I could vaguely see the world preparing itself to receive the sun's light. I could see the city, half-hidden, getting ready to intimidate us.

I could sense my mother's last dream in which she was kneeling at the feet of some man, begging to be the first for sacrifice. And I guessed that in another room María de Alava was jumping out of her bed and heading straight for my room.

My twin sister just stood there waiting for an answer. Despite the urge, something even stronger stopped me from saying anything to her. So, she started talking about the slippery mud all around the house. She said that her dreams forced her to go outside every night. I smiled, then I laughed out loud: I was seeing my mother in her. Attempting to blind me with jealousy, she had resorted to the mud that we loved to play in so much when we were infants. But my sister was only playing with mud, like before, and she had become aroused due to her prolonged abstinence – her painful and profound continence.

Even though her suffering was visible to me, there was nothing I could do for her. I wanted to laugh about the times my sister would punish us relentlessly. I wanted to see her as a young girl, but there was nothing like that about her, except for her existence clinging to me since before we came into being, or through our being. I felt for her like I felt for myself, but I was relentless in trying to overcome the barriers to our common existence.

She abruptly ended her parody. Inundated by peace, she confessed to me that she had spent three sleepless nights, three desperate nights, in which all she could do was think. At times she would manage to fall asleep for a few minutes, but then she would wake up assailed by broken images of her wretched dreams. She could barely remember them, but she managed to retain certain phrases or words that spurred her to understand their meaning.

She said she had heard an abundance of words, phrases, and commands in her brief dreams, and there were voices that spoke from the black recesses of darkness, clamoring for dead people she didn't know or couldn't remember. Those images enshrouded in darkness gave rise to snatches of shadows that she was unable to reconstruct in her sleeplessness. She said she wanted to go to sleep but her world of dreams only kept her awake.

All of a sudden she fell placidly but imperatively into a state of serenity, where she could perceive her mind giving in to her body, now triumphant. Her body shifted to seek repose; but then her brain would send shock waves through her body, creating spasms that startled her in bed.

After three sleepless nights, she couldn't discern what was real or unreal anymore or determine how much of her suffering was pure fantasy.

At times she would perceive that I was at her side like before, which would allow her to go to sleep. She thought the image of me would help her deceive the part of her that had turned against her, the same rebellious part that forced her to stretch out her hand and search for me among the rumpled sheets.

Her tired muscles quivered from extreme tension, her eyes burned as if sand had lacerated her corneas, and her thirst was unquenchable. She imagined the walls covered with warriors, whose blood would ooze from horrible slashes and drip from the armor. She imagined birds of prey encircling her, waiting for her to drop from dehydration.

She sought the light in order to banish those apparitions, but the clarity made the situation even worse. Menaced by her own presence, she saw herself imprisoned in the room, facing not only the absurdity of the objects surrounding her but also a feeling of loneliness that she couldn't withstand; for that, she suffered life's depravities. She preferred darkness where she could at least summon up someone or something but, invariably, darkness was nothing more than a mockery.

Her hearing also left her feeling strange. The house would

creak and she thought the walls were going to tumble down on top of her.

She imagined those walls containing some form of perverted humanity that she had managed to decipher in a surprisingly lucid state of mind. She would hear footsteps, groaning, and then someone would moan and laugh at the ceiling; there was murmuring in my parents' bedroom, words that proclaimed the indecency of their children. She could hear, ever so distinctly, bones banging sharply together, knees against knees, even my mother's skull becoming heated up as the bony mass began to resonate.

She could hear María de Alava talk in her dreams with such candor that it surprised her. Her melodious voice seemed to sing lightly, telling a story about goodness, where human beings were able to take advantage of the best they had to offer in order to donate it to the sadness of an inert rock. The voices in María de Alava's dreams proved that her own being was destroyed by perpetual, slashed wounds. She believed that my little sister dreamed that way in order to strengthen her martyrdom, always fleeing from the goodness that would elude her.

That third night, when she appeared in my room, was the culmination: she could bear no more. While murmurs, groans, and images superimposed themselves, she tried to leave. With surprising ease, she walked through the house to the door that opened easily and quietly.

Outside, the world seemed to sing with almighty strength, receiving her body in order to fuse it with the vitality of the earth. However, she understood that nothing was natural, only that the earth was constructing the ruse of a spectacle.

To her, the nights had become depersonalized, as the vagueness of her senses evaporated. She thought that the family was somewhere behind her and she was standing next to every

human species possible, while at the same time enjoying un-
limited expanses that made it possible to cast off her passion.

She wanted to test the coherence of her discovery and, without fully understanding what she was doing, she began to dig
for slimy worm larvae that lived in the soil. They would slip
out of her hands and she knew then she had overcome her fear
of death. Each worm was the inverted transformation of her
body, which some day would reach that inferior stage, moving
the species backwards.

Pity was her nocturnal celebration: pity for the worms, pity
for her eyeball sockets, pity for her skeleton that was growing
up haughtily but insensitively, sure that her flesh would cover
it forever.

She said she didn't have any idea how long she had been
digging in the dirt. Suddenly everything had ended and she
had to go to my room to eliminate the other unknown, for she
had already deciphered the meaning of her origin, the key to
which, she thought, involved me – not my parents.

She believed that our union as one could awaken in our
memory the real impact of our origin and the singular, non-
repeatable instant in which the organism decided on gesta-
tion. I had been a witness to her emergence to life and, therefore, I was key to the answer.

She said that when she stood in front of me, she knew that I
wasn't going to unlock the door. She told me she had already
sensed in me the fall toward a vulgar sex act. She had felt in me
jealousy, embarrassment, and fear; she pitied my small mind.

She declared with a certainty I'd never seen in her that I had
been living under delusion too long; she was tired of nourishing me, given that I had been confusing her with my mother,
not only for her milk but also for her limited and unstable
being. She repeated that she was tired of nourishing my life
and having to go around sweeping away mirages from the
desert that I had fabricated in my mind.

61

Although I could have stopped her, I let her go toward the door. I remained motionless for a few minutes, capitulating to pain. Everything took on a densely gray color with the first light of dawn.

Heedless of the house's silence, I left my room and walked directly to hers. I don't know what kind of reality motivated her repentance and the salty quality of her tears. I was interested only in her words, the same ones that negated what she had said, for she cursed her mind-altering insomnia, leading her to believe that I was her enemy.

MY MOTHER precipitated her own confinement, turned the universe upside down, reversed the flow of the waters, unearthed millenarian ruins, and revived war chants and putrefaction. My mother had committed adultery.

Ruthlessly, her act tore the family apart. My father's intense pain concerning what she had done not only astonished us but greatly embarrassed us like never before. This time a conqueror of flesh and bone had forced his way in, and my mother surrendered herself to lust on the edge of the city where, in a sordid room, she would conduct her visits.

My father was the laughingstock and he would watch her quiver without understanding the source of her mockery. The city also laughed at us.

My father found out without even trying. Haunted by the mockery, he felt compelled to confront the truth and he followed my mother to the exact place of her last tryst. He burst into the shabby room and in a quick glimpse was able to reconstruct every last rendezvous from which he had been excluded.

He thought vomiting would make him feel better and restore things to the way they were. When he saw a residue on the soaking bed slithering to the floor, he instantly perceived that he was crossing over into a nightmare.

He imagined my mother's nakedness inciting the other body to ecstasy. That vivid image triggered a flow of urine that gushed warmly down his legs, inundating him. Exuding tears and sweat, shivers and panic, he felt morally wounded, for a part of him died at that moment.

The gossip in the city emanated seemingly from his dead parents' mouths; they laughed at his new status. His old mother's agitation, now forgotten, resounded through time and traveled all the way back to that room, attacking the revelry of those women who had separated her from her world.

My mother was terrified to look at him. He took on the semblance of what an entire nation that was about to disappear would look like. Facing my father with her back to her lover, she was almost unrecognizable now; love and fear had enveloped her. She wanted to kneel down, but she had spent her energy and couldn't move. She thought about begging, but couldn't find the words to explain her guilt.

The intensity of her desire was overwhelming: she imagined herself being thrown savagely onto the soaking bed and possessed by my father while the ineffectual, already forgotten lover stood by and watched. The fervor of the passion invading her gave her a nuance that neither my father nor the conqueror of flesh had ever seen.

For a brief moment, the two of them looked at her enraptured, as a stranger belonging to someone else. In her were combined the looks of a prominent prostitute and a young, head-shaven novitiate about to enter the cloister. She also looked like some mentally deranged person who was receiving a lashing in order to quiet her down, or a beggar to whom, without reason, you would give a gold coin for charity. Her expression was the closest to what one might call a state of ecstasy; neither man could take his eyes off her, in spite of the fact that the situation that had brought them there bore no relation to the appearance that my mother had adopted at that moment.

Upon discovering the exact nature of her desire, my mother entered into an absolutely irreverent and mysterious state. To perceive it made her feel like she was truly being consumed by it.

My father possessed her flawlessly, with the perfection of pain and the force of jealousy, before the humiliated eyes of the paralyzed lover who was nothing more than a part of the decor. Impelled by the illuminating frenzy of her brain, she became a vision of surrender, sustained by the penurious bones of the human species.

She thought she heard the lacerated, explosive voice of a black woman who, chanting a solemn hymn, opened her legs to guide her to ecstasy.

She understood that pleasure embodied a combination of infinite dissipation and cathartic excesses of the forsaken in the world; she was therefore able to pay homage to the dispossessed, the conceivers of sin, those guilty of crime, those induced to lust.

Submissive, her journey took her along a clearly cosmic yet personal path. My father and her lover could observe, perplexed, the contortions of climax dominating her face.

My mother lay back exhausted and, for a few seconds, seemed to have fainted. My father picked her up and carried her outside into the cold.

As they walked through the city, they were both buried deep in their own thoughts and emotions. At one point my mother attempted to get close to him but he rejected any contact with her by walking ahead. Acquiescing, she followed behind, trying to imagine not only what was going to happen during the next few hours but also what kind of future was in store for her.

My father walked along, engulfed by diverse sensations. Part of him had already forgotten what had happened. When he looked at her out the corner of his eye, her behavior still seemed especially impossible to him and, at the same time, he could feel that his pride wanted to destroy her, even kill her.

He felt like he didn't even know her and he was curious to discover her thoughts, her every sensation; he was irritated by the urgency with which she would narrate a new, comprehensive version – reprehensible but personal – of her life. He wanted to reduce her to exhaustion and, once he was satisfied, throw her out into the streets, letting the cold, hunger, and disease finish her off.

He sensed, however, that he wasn't going to abandon her; he was hoping, rather, that with the time they had left in life, he could erase what had happened. However, he was able to observe that both of them had been given the privilege of descending, step by step, into hell.

WE DECIDED that confinement would shield us from the embarrassment and humiliation. Decaying over time by the confinement, I tried to remain distant from the rest of my house's inhabitants, who continually acted like transvestites in order to conclude their perversity. My crestfallen twin sister adopted a stance of penury, just like the others, amid the vertigo of pretense.

During that atrocious inaugural period, the family turned to every kind of indulgence possible, except for the penumbra that horrified my twin sister. We kept everything turned on – neon lights, fluorescent lights, candles – in order to shun the darkness that could pervert us into solitary practices censured by Order.

In our spacious quarters we reduced our food consumption to a minimum. María de Alava distributed the food to us with

65

her customary grace. We would frequently curl up against the walls to ward off a crushing mental massacre. We sensed that the dimension of the crime had expanded so that it formed an intangible thick layer, leaving us more and more insecure.

Permeated by my father's metallic voice and the constant lashing out of his pride, we hardly spoke to each other.

My mother's sallow and suppurating skin was covered with shame. We became alarmed and panicked. As time was becoming critical, I assented to deposit the confession with my twin sister.

## 2. I HAVE A TERRIBLY CONSTRAINED HAND

MY TWIN BROTHER adopted the name María Chipia and, like a transvestite, became a virgin, for a virgin could predict the birth. He predicted it. He predicted it for me. He proclaimed it.

A strange fertilization took place in the room when the seminal residue trickled out and I felt the remainder sting like a whiplash.

'Oh, no! Oh, no!' we said in unison upon perceiving the catastrophe that had beset us. An archaic, hybrid, asphyxiating compromise evolved, plunging us into apprehension.

I decided to entrust María de Alava with the child we had just conceived. I decided to do it from that very first moment as an offering and a pardon for the family guilt.

(The child was already terribly deformed.)

María de Alava, who had been present during the act, mocked us with a chant that praised our union and said:

'This sudaca family needs my help. This sudaca child will need my help more than anyone else.'

The act was concluded. To understand it was to repeat it and, thus, to erase it. Assailing his virginity that he called evil – it signified evil – María Chipia curled up on the floor and licked the dust, naked, like a child of God. Angrily, I struggled with the blood, also like a child of God.

(The child was on its way in the midst of the melancholic peacefulness of disapproval.)

I bent over praying to be pardoned for my telluric sexuality. María Chipia and María de Alava invoked the eroticism of the masses. I was one of them. After the lustful act, I fell into frightening remission, dispossessed of form and body, but morally fractured.

'WHAT HAVE you done? What have you done?'

My father's voice deafened the room, brutally.

We were frightened, frightened out of our wits. My father, old and cruel, implored, blamed, and swore at my mother. My mother, now old and obscene, realized that his hatred was sacred and she acquiesced as her infected body hurled a scornful grimace toward our bodies, now dissipated from passion and run through with ancient, maternal adultery.

We saw that virility had apparently maintained its correct and equally harmful comportment. Like twins descendent, we were conceiving our own autistic progeny in the midst of family obstinacy. A somatically paired progeny with intimately coupled chromosomes. Totally unique.

María Chipia wasn't the splendid young boy he used to be; he wasn't disdainful or ambivalent. He hid his face from my parents and accused me of contaminating him with atavistic and venereal resentment.

María Chipia began to have convulsions not unlike an epileptic fit; clots formed along the commissures of his nerves. María de Alava and I didn't assist him, we just lowered our heads. My father's anger finished tearing my membrane.

(I found out that the child would be disfigured upon birth.)

I strained my head toward María Chipia who, imitating my father, could barely speak during one of his convulsions:

'What have we done? What have we done?'

We bowed our heads as my mother would walk past us, incessantly dripping blood ever since her adultery. My father ordered her to abandon the chamber. I anguished over their wretchedness.

Rubbing his mouth with his hands, María Chipia said:

'I want María de Alava to dance a tribute to me.'

MARÍA CHIPIA and I know we were born on a day that God was sick. Obsessed, he repeats untiringly, 'I am an honorable sudaca, I am an honorable sudaca,' while the syllables split apart against the walls of the house.

During the day, opacity emanates from his painted eyes. His nocturnal expression is one of agony. He calls to me and pulls me against his bare chest. He asks me to do something new, try novel positions; he asks me to contemplate the possibility of committing obscenities. His bare chest touches mine and, further away, speaking of desire, his genitals are throbbing.

He possesses me all night long. María Chipia possesses me throughout the night while my parents, standing at the windows, observe us through the cracks. It was difficult to do – most difficult – with them peering at us, but each time we were unable to avoid those terrifyingly intimate moments together.

María de Alava orders me to describe the act. I obey her, acquiescing to the futility of my articulation. I write my experiences down on paper and María Chipia draws my parents' position.

My mother's embarrassment surrounds us, enveloping us in a profuse blue wake.

María de Alava asks me to describe the act once again:

'María Chipia possessed me all night long.'

'While my parents were watching?'

'Yes, from the very center of their pupils.'

María Chipia, overcome by heat, doesn't stop possessing me; his errant soul filled the cracks, blocking the vision of his parents while they banged their heads against the window.

In the darkness of the night, we played at being twins. Primordial, intimate, and sultry, the game was abundant with secretions. We were extenuated by dawn, but we had made sure the child's sex was clearly identifiable.

María Chipia asks me to expose my secret.

I violate it by saying:

'I want to create a creature that is terribly and scandalously sudaca.'

I MOVED voluptuously. Oh, yes. Oh, yes. Voluptuously.

María Chipia never stopped crying. María de Alava, fat, envious, seething, sitting on a stool; she waited for the family to explode and for our guilt to be forgotten. I tried to keep things going, maybe learn how to be a midwife, but I hallucinated images: a dangerous scalpel and ordinary bushes would appear in my mind.

A voice pierced my brain, a voice engraved on the tragic neural void, foretelling the moment of birth that was already lodged in the dominant left lobe. The voice insulted my genital opening.

Hazy, distant, stupefied, I drew near María de Alava's hunched figure and begged her for a meeting later on, much later on, I told her, a preliminary hearing in order to attenuate the guilt.

Still slumped over, she agreed:

'Later.'

My twin brother overheard me arranging the meeting which excluded him; already physiologically weak, he became neurotic, a perfect example of psychosis. He subsequently performed a beautiful ritual in which he turned arid white.

His hair fell down to his shoulders, his eyeballs revolved in their sockets, and his skull practically exploded (he hadn't slept in two nights). María Chipia danced and danced, obliterating his feelings; his cheeks slowly took on an affected, artificial rosy glow.

Outside the room, our parents were insulting us. They were on a rampage. María Chipia staged his last presentation of an apparent speech impairment; he appeared to be suffering from aphasia, but his rictus was the crowning moment of pain as he was unable to modulate the complexity of his name. His high theatricality converged into an ideal, taciturn scheme.

María de Alava and I left him alone to revel in all his magnitude. Before we left, María Chipia murmured into my ear that the child would be deformed at birth.

MARÍA DE ALAVA heard my confession. I was extremely tired and I let my head slump down.

She remained erect, fearless and menacing: she was still seething.

'María de Alava,' I said to her, 'abort your contempt and listen to my request. Put yourself in my degraded, worthless situation.'

She waited impassively – absorbed, aloof, adversarial.

'María de Alava,' I said, 'our bad sudaca behavior is to blame for this horrendous catastrophe.'

She put her index finger to her lips, moistened it with her tongue and then spit on the stool.

'There's no way out,' she said. 'You should seek refuge in my brother.'

'Don't mention his name; he's my obsession and fear.'

'You will have to confront me at my best,' she said. 'I will conquer your bodies from inside my own.'

'You have exceeded the limits of necessity,' I told her. 'I want to dispel this urgency.'

'Do you abhor your swollen belly?' she asked.

María de Alava looked at me like an inquisitor. I described that instant of the terrible fissure and my astonishment at the flowing blood. I told her, in fact, that I was unable to escape my propensity to drowsiness. I also told her that my pregnancy needed a new neon halo to make me stand out.

She forged the tube for me.

María de Alava gave me the present: a blue, shining circle that matched my earrings and my hairdo, and complemented my face, now sullen from the movements of the creature inside.

I talked to her. I talked about myself, about my mother's lacerated body that was being destroyed by continence. I celebrated the inevitability of our original sin. I thought the bonfire was close by, but I managed to ward it off; I finished by explaining the specific openings of my swaddled and firm genitals.

I TALKED to María de Alava straightforwardly, fearing nothing.

'My mother is covered with personal wounds.'

'Repeat that,' she said.

'She still has adultery on her mind.'

Consumed by the curse of fecundation, my systemic body was hurting, just as my methodical brain pained me in front of her.

They were aching, the two organisms ached.

The entire room became disquieting. The confusion created a large obstacle between us. In our emaciated, contorted faces, our eyes didn't notice anything specifically, but in the end my turmoil was like a laser. My twin brother perturbed me: it was his exasperating calmness. We discovered that the moment of confession was drawing near. We discovered it together and we attempted to delay it. We were exhausted.

María de Alava, half-dazed, prepared herself. I planted myself directly in front of her. Feeling miserable, I provided a hierarchical inventory of my iniquities. From my partially closed eyes I could see María Chipia dancing, provoking in me an acute psychic catastrophe. While he danced, pain pierced my eyes.

Even so, I braced myself:

'I must forget about the dancing.'

I could feel the creature dancing inside me, testing me. The confession lost its validity.

'But I must still reduce my mother's shame.'

(I continued with unnerving lucidity.)

'Now the family has been contaminated with apathy. The voices inside me are telling me to sharpen our discontent, make it the sudaca type, red and avaricious like blood.'

María de Alava raised her head and stood up from the stool (the stool could barely contain her obesity). She indicated she was ready for tomorrow. Dazed by the wait, I would have to prop up my mother's body, which was alive and aroused.

Near dawn, my mother, who was next to me, murmured:

'It's mother-of-pearl. The thread runs through my silk panties.'

I HAD a premonition that my siblings were moving quietly through the house in order to find an opportune place, dragging along with them the force of anarchy. When I heard their bodies rub together, I stayed behind.

I remained attentive in order to bear their guilt, and mine, carrying the ancient, degrading sudaca humanity on my back. Falling. Falling. Explosive.

That night María de Alava became terrorized by the night. For María Chipia it was a time of pleasure: he was overcome by spasms, trapped by disjointed movements, waiting for the questions of his terrible inquisitor and clinging to himself as if he were going to vanish.

My mother: begging for clemency and peace for the family. My father: assailed by insomnia, revealed disturbing assumptions as he spoke. María de Alava would call them the 'abstract elders,' but they love us, they love us with the same intensity as before the fall.

When? When was the fall?

I ventured to ask María de Alava, but she silenced me from the other room. My mother took advantage of my confusion, making me continue to prop her up with my strained bones in a more inappropriate position to my organism. I would be trapped all night long.

I saw the dawn, already crippled and impersonal. María

de Alava appeared wearing the marks of a penitent on her arms after María Chipia would touch her, yes, touch her. And I, having to care for my mother so they could scorn aberration, became a martyr.

I fell into a state of contagious somnolence. My mother, scratching at my back, said:

'Divine. Divine. María Chipia's battered ego. The wounded opening of women.'

'YOU LOOK imposing, María de Alava,' I said to her.

'Don't flatter me,' she answered. 'Don't even try to give me a moment of pleasure.'

My frenzy awoke a reckless hunger in María de Alava: she began to chew on tiny stems and pieces of bread. She would bite her fingernails, pale with hunger.

Suddenly, light filtered in. Its white virulence startled María de Alava, who then returned to her chair.

The light made me feel like confessing and I was stimulated to new revelations:

'We have done terrible and outlandish things.'

Amid outbursts of laughter, my sister said:

'There is never enough for the sudaca stigma. Look at my father's defeated brow. During these years, my mother hasn't stopped bleeding.'

'María de Alava,' I said, 'I need you urgently to help me decipher my last vision, a terrifying, deceptive, threatening vision to the child.'

My sister buried her face in her hands; she said a tribute could free us permanently from the most powerful nation in the world, which had put a curse on us. She considered stretching canvas with phosphorescent stripes across the front of the house. She said the most powerful nation changed names every century, hiding in new clothing. She asserted that only brotherhood could propel that nation into crisis.

I thought about the need for a tribute. A simple and popular homage. We had to respond to the most powerful nation in the world.

MARÍA CHIPIA keeps going around looking for me, and I'm hoping for some gesture of love from him, a sign of love, a shriek of love. There is no place for us now and, as the last resort, he asks me to sing to him.

He asks me to sing the most obscene song that has ever been sung. Beseeching, he turns red as he squats in the far reaches of the room. His face painted a golden color, he looks at me straight on, hoping to compete with the neon stars that twinkle in splendor above.

While he howls and contorts, he asks me to satiate him and to act according to our indivisible brotherhood, created in the most destructive love song of all time.

He howls and contorts in order to escape from the humiliation and the fall of our family. I think I'll sing him a song of senility, a terribly senile and tiring song, in order to clear away the unknowns that threaten us like a sharp knife in the darkness of the fetal waters.

I confess to him my inclination toward sin and, pervertedly, I open myself up as if I had been holding back my desires forever. Agape, I hope my teeth separate from my gums so that he can confront my sinister skull. I lick him like a child who is gestating inside a ragged and emaciated mother.

I curse myself and curse my song, flogging myself like a whore who spends the night in a cell of men condemned to death.

Knowing the past and bold about the present, I want all the sleepless nights and worms that devour my brain to embellish my song. And I want my brain to be there as well.

(I also sing for the child who is already suffering from an irreversible process.)

Finally, the tempestuous zones of our bodies come into contact at the moment of an intense sexual tremor. For many hours, the song deadens the contempt we feel toward our sudaca race.

WE ARE fiercely prepared for extinction. A small, enlightened, forsaken family. María de Alava, possessed by obsession, orders me to kneel.

'It's impossible for me to confess on my knees now,' I tell her, 'I'm permanently nauseated. To look at you from the floor turns my stomach.'

'Don't dawdle, don't wander. Let's examine the last article.'

'I'm guilty, María de Alava. I'm the one who clamored for sin. The more I arched my body, the deeper the pleasure.'

María de Alava takes notes. She lists the charges against me that become too excessive for a single execution. If I smother myself, María de Alava will drown the child. He or she will be free. But our house is under siege because of the voracity of the most powerful nation in the world and it will not last either.

(The child is suffering convulsions in my belly.)

My father is weeping in the other room, weeping for my mother's shame.

'My father has turned into an unbearable voyeur,' I tell her.

I tell her my latest dream. A dream with disjointed figures. I explain that in my dream, I managed with difficulty to make out a hand, but the nails separated from the fingers and the fingers disappeared, severed from the palms. She explained that it was a dream about my stubbornness and, before leaving, she said:

'You have to learn that pleasure is purulence, and the idea of war an orgy.'

To María Chipia. Handsome. Handsome and brotherly.

I AM a victim of a tumultuous political plot against our race. They persecute us with the force of their scorn. Now my mother sleeps on top of me, exhausted after having performed a tribute to the most powerful nation on earth. She believes my father is in collusion with that nation and that we are the carrion. She has confessed to me that her devotion to hedonism opened the way to this disaster that consolidates all plagues into one. She believes that the child is a plague and that his or her arrival will bring uncertainty, which is exactly what my father is waiting for in order to destroy her. She thinks María de Alava is conspiring with my father.

(My mother doesn't like María de Alava.)

Clinging to me, she told me in secret that my sister arouses my father's flesh and this, frankly, is what I want to talk to you about. When my mother confirmed that they were playing the whole game, I thought I would never forgive you, because I thought you were part of the plot. The other afternoon I caught you by surprise looking enraptured through a crack in the window and, when I asked you what you were looking at, you answered, lying to me, that you were measuring the density of light. I won't forgive you, because you still fear my old father, who hasn't defeated his virility. You still fear the softness of silk. You are afraid of my sister and my mother, and it seems like the multiplicity of your dreams is taking you closer and closer to the most famous and powerful nation in the world.

But it is I, reading and translating the sexual activities of this family, who knew exactly when the members would speak of possession. María de Alava didn't do anything but barely respond to the sickly pleas of my mother, who pitied her meanness.

You were the only one who delayed our encounter. Since you are myself, I know everything you know – despite the distances; but we both know which is the only way to delay our extinction and the humiliation of our race.

This has exhausted me and it provokes continual fear. Right now my mother is deeply asleep with her buttocks up against mine. Later on, near dawn, I will go to you so you can soothe my mind. After daylight comes and my mother wakes up, I'll return to her side and she won't be aware of what will have happened between us.

MARíA CHIPIA crawls on the floor looking for some money in order to leave the house. He scratches desperately in the corners, insisting loudly on the existence of the coins.

His last torn silk shirt makes him look like a hysterical beggar, ranting out of failure. He crushes every insect hiding in the niches of just about any orifice. His fingers, caked with the residue, managed to make me pity him for an instant.

I approach him in order to lick him and he puts his fingers down my throat, causing me to vomit violently. I feel the child, now alarmed, make a strange movement inside me.

'You will be present for the birth,' I say to him. 'You will be here for the birth.'

Entangled in his persistent cowardice, and accusing me of having a malignant memory, he hits me. I step back from his fists and scream a carefully elaborated scream:

'You will be here, nevertheless.'

He continues clawing for the means of his escape, more exhausted than ever, and, from above, I observe how he voluntarily evokes pathos.

'I'm going to leave this house,' he murmurs. 'I'm going to abandon you,' he says.

I managed to seize the last bit of money left in the house that was hidden in my father's secret pants pocket. As I grasped it tightly, I could clearly see freedom.

Fascinated by his contortions, I continue to watch his useless struggle. His muscles contract, making his skin bulge through the torn silk. His thighs and heels squeeze together out of anxiety over the money.

Finally, he falls to the ground and a hollow hatred for my belly emanates from his eyes. I offer him my deformity, responding to a minimal gesture of his that he quickly interprets. My reaction is an invitation to share my composure.

As he approaches me, his hand brushes my side, his eyes swell with tears and his makeup starts to run. I touch his feverish forehead and, in doing so, my hand seemingly touched his brain because the chaos of his thoughts propels me backwards.

'I will leave this house,' I say out loud. 'After the birth, I will leave this house.'

The coins dig into the palm of my hand, creating a slight fissure in my soul.

WE ARE resting on our sides on the floor. María Chipia talks to me about the benefits of death and the importance of sacrifice. He describes the most famous and powerful nation on earth as if it were a phosphorescent skull that emits fine, almost imperceptible rays. He says he has seen them from the window, infiltrating the city. He asserts that a large space for death is being created outside. He invites me to leave the house and to seek out our place in death.

I talk to him again about sudaca brotherhood and how our power could destroy that nation of death. I talk to him about the child. I describe my most recent premonitions. I tell him that I need to rest because the child also wants to abandon me. I begin to loathe the complacency of my genitals.

While María Chipia dozes at my side, I faithfully follow the outline of the child, who has just deciphered the path of the labyrinth. I can feel the movement, the head pointing downward, but closing my thighs tightly doesn't lessen my horror.

Now that the child wants to abandon me, I know the only thing I have left is the insistence of María Chipia's body, who is also fleeing from me, like me from myself, as I'm pursuing him out of terror of pursuing and destroying myself in the obscure hostility of my own being.

I feel surrounded by fugitive bodies, by bits and pieces of fugitives that antagonize our imprisoned origins. I feel wounded by the bodies that have capitulated to the conditions of their defeat. I feel unworthy of having a body.

Serenely, I get up from the floor and look for María de Alava. I find her staring strangely at her feet. Realizing that I had approached her, she says:

'A dance, we must dance a tribute.'

The child, who listens but resists, moves inside me with surprising harmony. I imagine corn, wheat, willow groves. The three of us dance until dawn.

WE ARE in the coldest season and it assaults us with ferocious aggressiveness. Because of the cold I become dangerously lethargic. Only the child makes a few slight, torpid movements. María Chipia, turning bluish, tells me he has prepared a lecture that will keep us awake. I know he has prepared a lecture that will allow him to leave the house, but I'm unable to expose his desires. María de Alava makes a gesture of displeasure; my parents, too far gone now, are completely out of touch.

Outside, bonfires are being lit around the city, surrounding it in flames. The reflection taints the windows red and we become submerged in dense, fluctuating shadows. María de Alava goes to the window and her lips form meaningless words.

My father opens his eyes and says the plague has arrived. My mother nods in agreement and also says the plague has arrived. I sit down on the threshold of martyrdom. María Chipia practices, he practices a redeeming lecture about our guilt, a lecture in which he reconciles the burden of our story. He practices his lecture and through his words he modulates the severity of our deeds and the dignity of our bodies.

He redeems my mother's sexual faults in a tone that fills me with shame. Throughout his essay, one can perceive the true intentions of his words. But it's too late and his gullibility surprises me. In his second presentation, he imitates a bold and convincing lecturer, invoking a conciliatory and crushing surrender.

Utilizing all the voices that inhabit him, María Chipia is preparing a lecture dedicated to himself; it's a lecture dedicated to himself and to the child. The flow of the primeval waters could be heard in one of his voices and I felt a surge of warmth surround me.

Outside, the young sudacas are hovering around the bonfires and a familiar sound fills my ears: the hooves of horses. I hear horses' hooves.

TODAY, María Chipia and I have eaten alone. A ritual. We planned a simile of a meal in the most convenient way possible. After there was nothing left, we gestured competitively, down to the slowness of our chewing. With the prolonged absence of food, we ate as if it were unnecessary, trying to disregard the hunger pangs.

We talked.

At first, he talked, swamped by suspicion. He spoke as a deceptive stranger trying to seduce me with an intense look of intimacy. I also played the role of the stranger and my face yielded to the pose that I invented. We were play-acting, and we played at creating an adult couple.

When boredom set it, I took on another role equally false and banal. I imbued myself with distance, bracing myself with an aloof gaze and ironic gestures. Submerged in the distance, I constructed for him an inner world in which he didn't recognize me, the inner world that he had always hoped for – warm, pliable, full of orifices, hoping that he would be able to destroy me. I represented the most fragile and destructive part of the adult couple.

It was relatively easy to create a common and well-known mystery; similarly, it was easy to observe the pleasures of destruction. I let myself fall prey to a weakness that, in truth, I didn't possess; and I talked, I talked about a succession of terrors that were out of control, and I prepared to be abandoned.

Slowly, the rhythm of that simile of a meal put me face to face with our true character. When hunger was upon us, our capacity for parody was over. The fragments of a desire that didn't sustain us anymore exploded and our desires began to devour each other. The battle pitted jealousy against jealousy and, for an instant, envy colored our cheeks.

Envious of the child, María Chipia assailed me with his keen animosity and, I, envious of his flat stomach, took refuge in the advantages of his condition. We ate the leftovers. Close to each other, we surrendered to the true couple that we were, without any more secrecy than cannibalism. I escorted myself to my maternal corner as if there was still a pinch of integrity left between us. That night desire mortified my brain.

TERRIBLY enlarged, I'm straddling María Chipia, trying to obtain pleasure. It comes and goes. The pleasure comes and goes. When it comes, it comes with oblivion and the climax of pleasure fills the void. It totally permeates me and María Chipia intensifies his movements because he knows I'm about to have an orgasm.

But something prevents it, something annoying and incisive. I lose it. Even though I still cling to the after-effects, there's nothing more important than to recuperate it in order to forget it. I fall into a state of acute desperation, talking in fragments, demanding more movement from María Chipia and the continuity that I require.

Although I know my face is distorted by effort, I fix my gaze upon him – underneath me, stretched out, supporting my obesity and pushing hard, in spite of my weight.

His face is also convulsed, but fearing my hatred, he holds back. His face has a singular look – his lips are parted, he's panting, and his gaze, even though he's looking at me, focuses far beyond, lost in his own pleasure.

It's been three times now during the course of this evening, and I have even lost the individual nature of my own smell; for María Chipia's smell exudes from the sopping pores of my body. It doesn't stop. Even after obtaining pleasure the first three times, the urge to continue isn't consummated. My anguish unabated, I command María Chipia to begin anew.

He touches me according to the urgency of my needs and I achieve it immediately. I manage to climax immediately, despite my interfering, outstretched legs.

Half of the heat that I feel comes from the hottest and most dangerous part that I possess, and the other half comes from María Chipia, which he introduces with his thrusts. Even though I know I'll fully attain it, I will do it again because my anguish continues to rise to a rhythmic pulse that I've reached before. María Chipia knows it and he takes pleasure in my affliction. He obtains his heat from me and from my face, which has completely lost any semblance of symmetry.

I let myself fall until my tongue touches his and, this time, the child doesn't separate us. The force of my hatred and my satisfaction compels me to lick him, and I'm afraid María Chipia won't be able to do it again.

I'M SPRAWLED out on my side with my swollen belly resting on the floor. Its size frightens me. Beside me, María Chipia desperately penetrates for pleasure. I don't care about his rhythmical attacks, and his corporeal movements are lost in my memory. I don't give him pleasure and I don't feel sorry for myself.

My nose, mouth, and ears need no attention; except for thirst, I have no cravings. I sense that at any moment the child is going to undertake the journey of escape. Hurting me, the child will leave by the same channel as the one of conception. I will lose both channels and be wounded forever.

María Chipia is looking for me to find a way out. The other morning when I asked him about it, he looked at me as if he didn't understand what I was talking about; but he did understand, and that same afternoon he possessed me more out of wickedness than necessity.

He wants to give the child a way out so he can leave himself. Due to my extreme corporeality, I am too weary to stop them. I know that a critical night is just beginning because my blood pressure has shot up. Nausea has increased, and I feel dehydrated. I haven't told María Chipia yet. I know he has been anxiously awaiting these symptoms because he has put on his most outlandish dress. With his head wrapped in silk, barefooted, eyes laden with mascara, gleaming eyebrows, and painted lips, I realize he is waiting for the moment of celebration. I pretend not to show any signs, but he seems to know that I'm in a precarious state.

I let him attack me from behind – even though María de Alava is tossing and turning not far away; even though I can feel their eyes, my parents have not stopped peering through the crack in the old window. Although I know we are perpetuating a sudaca stigma, I continue dauntlessly, looking for a way out myself.

I'm thinking about a new tribute. My parents sob next to the heavy, final rasping of María Chipia. I get up.

I ask María Chipia to gather the family together, telling him I'll spend the entire night preparing a tribute.

'The whole night?' he asks.

A sudden asthma attack forces me to cover myself with my kerchief.

THE NAUSEA. The pain. Constant nausea and pain, startling dreams and pain all over again. I am crushed by the swelling. The swelling is about to kill me. It alters my heartbeat, infects my kidneys, obstructs my hearing. My swollen eyelids have clogged my tear ducts and the humidity has clouded my vision. The tendons in my legs seem as if they are going to snap from my weight. The pain knows no truce. Congestion ascends my spine. Allergies. The swelling of allergies.

Swollen breasts. The pain of the milk. The child, an accomplice with the rest of the family, attacks me from within. I have incubated another enemy and I'm the only one who knows the magnitude of hatred. My head. In my head, I conceive confusing dreams that are shot through with vast expanses of doubt. Doubts about the child saunter through my swelling brain. Through pain, I learn to identify not only all the nooks and crannies of my body, but also the organic fury with which punishment is executed. My inflamed eyes witness a diffuse reality.

In order to escape from a decisive ending, I now conceive a dream that could defeat the violence of my body and destroy our sickness. At the opposite end of pleasure, I discover an equally diffuse territory that palpitates and turns me inward.

Malaise and engorgement induce this constant pain that pierces my bones, one after the other, so that now I can't even close my hand. I can only hear upsetting sounds that make me dizzy; the slightest creak is a blow to the stomach and any scream becomes a stampede in my head: my head, my temples, my eye sockets, my rotten teeth, my asthma, the burning in my breasts. My asthma, asphyxiation. The rasping of asthma. My soul under the microscopic eye of the family. With the slightest cough, the asthma begins and the child withdraws, terrified by an asthmatic future, the asthmatic soul of the child.

In order to escape from a decisive ending, I open myself up to the pain and neutralize myself. From within this new system, the child and I settle on a somatic agreement.

MARÍA DE ALAVA demands an answer.

'It'll be at dawn,' I tell her. 'The birth will be at dawn.'

She seems tired on interrogating me and by her expression I can tell she is suffering from prolonged fasting. My parents, covered with blankets in the corner of the room, insult us, now desperate because of hunger. They insult the birth. My mother talks crudely about her orifice; she compares it to ours and provokes my father to join in.

My father, ravenous with hunger, evokes the exactitude of the orifice, and his ulcerated mouth imitates an enormous vagina. My mother laughs and immediately dozes off.

María de Alava, unperturbed, stares at me.

'It will be at dawn,' I repeat.

By repeating it, I repeat the uncertainty of my affirmation. María de Alava settles down to wait. With irony, she anticipates the effect of her words:

'We are leaving this house,' she says. 'My parents and I will leave this house. Now that the city has stopped gossiping, I have prepared our departure. Now you people will be able to enjoy the full extent of your sudaca stigma.'

Incredulous, I search her eyes for contradiction. It doesn't exist. They will leave the house and we will inherit the severity of the walls and the cracks of family guilt. By abandoning the house, they will make more space and my body will become even more grotesque.

Still incredulous, I begin to understand that María de Alava, after all these years, has spoken the truth. To think that her words are sincere, after so many years, gives me the strength to resist abandonment and the abandonment of the brotherhood. Those who are left are the child and María Chipia, the ones who represent the limit of the invention of my body, my brutally punished body, my body punished because of the compulsion to duplicate myself, this body altered by the certainty of death.

At dawn, when the family abandons the house, I will be alone in great sorrow. The dawn that I was vaguely perceiving as the birth – or the genesis between darkness and light, night and day – was their departure.

AS MARÍA de Alava and my parents were leaving the house and, after they had barely crossed the threshold, María Chipia penetrated me from the front, causing me to bleed. The spurting blood paralleled my pain, but the blood, as it covered my parents' tracks, was the best tribute that María Chipia, the child, and I could give to losing our family. Still bleeding, I didn't dare get up. I remained motionless on the floor. I just stayed there, observing my defenseless, naive brother and his painful apathy.

I also discovered my innocence, sustained by this immutable, ambiguous occurrence. The certainty of my innocence pushed me to the edge of insurrection and I felt worthy of the property that we had so violently inherited.

We inherited the house and the lust in the house that, intermittently, invaded us. It invaded me and, despite the blood, I protected myself by taking an obscene position in order to beg María Chipia to help me conquer my feeling of rage.

That day we didn't ask each other for a truce. During the act, my searing clarity of the day dissipated, and the night, more benign but real, stimulated my imagination. Although the child was suffering, we could offer no help. I couldn't do anything because from day to night, I had to tend to the demands of my sudaca blood. I urgently needed that pleasure now more than anything else in life.

In the end, astraddle him, I was able to lose all sense of time as the border dissolved between outside and inside, and María Chipia became incorporated into my neuronic being. In perfect and singular fashion, we spent from dawn to dusk finding each other until we became fused. The child was suffering and we integrated that suffering into ourselves without guilt, without anxiety, and without evil.

It was a tribute to the sudaca species. It was a manifesto. It was a dynastic celebration of the coming of the child who that day was able to experience the immense power of his or her parents: their hatred. Isolated in a distinctly organic sphere, the child experienced the parents' most charming attributes.

I HAVE FALLEN into a state of semiparalysis. My swollen body prevents me from moving and I'm incapable of attending to María Chipia, who is wandering about the house, feverish and starving. His reddened face becomes even more inflamed with the glow in his eyes. His bloodshot eyes seem lacerated by the light. We are thirsty but water doesn't satisfy us. María Chipia complains of the infection, he complains about the light, and ridicules his bones that have become thin knives, cutting him from the inside. I raise my hand and touch his cheeks and forehead; they are burning, wet with sweat.

I'm frightened that it's contagious, I'm frightened another sickness will befall me, so I ask him to lie down in another room; he refuses, saying hunger has precipitated the fever. But I know it's the abandonment – the family exodus – that has instilled the fever in the house.

Immobilized, I search for a way to cure María Chipia because I will need his help when the child is born. While he murmurs something about the hostility of the city, I remember that we still own the water and that water helps to fight dogs' fever. Like feverish, starving sudaca dogs, we need to pour the water on top of us in order to get rid of the infection and, even though I don't have any fever, I can feel it closing in, now that my mother has abandoned us like dogs. The darkness of abandonment and the absence of the pack stimulate my muscles to act. I sit up, in spite of my swelling, which is part water and part fat.

With compassion, María Chipia watches my heroic movements. I look at him as if he were the last thing I owned; clinging to his equivocal beauty, I say to him:

'Water! You must conduct a ritual with water.'

I helped him undress and praised the harmony of his body. I clapped in unison with his weak chant, poured the water over his body and, when the fever had subsided, we were fatigued; soon, we slept, surrounded by my ample bulk.

'ARE YOU cold, María Chipia? Thirsty? Do you want anything?'

'I want to know more about the city. Do you even remember the city? Do you remember the construction going on?'

'Ah, yes. The construction workers. The young, seminaked sudacas. And the beggars. They would chase me through the streets. The young sudacas always wanted something from me.'

'What did they want? That was always our fantasy.'

'It wasn't a fantasy. Once a young sudaca stuck out his hand and when I put a coin in it, he refused it. I can still see his sunken eyes, like yours. Perhaps it was a fever. He spoke about the brotherhood. He talked a long time about it.'

'I saw a wheat field outside the city. A field full of wheat stalks swaying in the wind, a field of stalks planted by the blind children at my mother's shelter. I'll take you to that field and as you sway in the breeze, you can give birth.'

'I saw a sordid house where my mother was swaying also, in the darkness that seemed to blind you. I didn't see it, but I imagined it. I can imagine it right this instant. And my father, terrified of the city. I can imagine the plagues and the fever. The child will not be born in order to replenish the garbage.'

'But . . . the corn, the wheat, the willow groves?'

'The child will not come into this world to be despised, he will not come demanding something for nothing. Children fight to be born every moment. What will we do, María Chipia? What will we do?'

'Take me! Take me! Take me!'

OUTSIDE, the devastated city grumbles and is given to useless chatter. With the hope that money will fall from the sky, every kind of rhetorical discourse is heard; like fireflies, the words disappear in weak flashes. The myopic, miserly city doles out the destinies of its sudaca inhabitants. The city, palsied, broken down and irritable, old and greedy, begins to falter.

Their voices waver, especially the old and greedy, as they squabble over the money that falls from the sky but vanishes into thin air. They sell the wheat, the corn, and the willow groves for nothing, while the young sudacas who planted them look on. Sweat is for sale. Frantic merchants shriek at the buyers, who astutely lower the prices to buy up everything, including the sellers themselves. The money from the sky returns to the sky and the sellers even sell what doesn't belong to them.

The city, fallen into collapse, is already a fiction. Only the name of the city remains, because everything else has been sold on the open market. Amid the anarchy of supply and demand, the last items are auctioned off, amid accusations of sham and fraud.

The money that falls from the sky stimulates not only urban fraud but also the false rhetoric about planting a hoax in the fields, which is already sold and now belongs to someone else. The money from the sky enters directly through the sex organs, and the ancient voices surrender to wanton adultery. Adultery has perverted the city; the city prostitutes itself, giving itself away at any price to any bidders. The transaction is about to conclude and the contempt for the sudaca race is clearly printed on the money falling from the sky.

Far away, in a house abandoned to brotherhood, between April 7 and 8, diamela eltit, assisted by her twin brother, gives birth to a baby girl. The sudaca baby will go up for sale.

# IN THE LATIN AMERICAN WOMEN WRITERS SERIES

To order or obtain more
information on these or other
University of Nebraska Press titles,
visit *www.nebraskapress.unl.edu*.

CPSIA information can be obtained at www.ICGtesting.com
Printed in the USA
BVOW011454021211

277347BV00001B/26/P